THE AXMAN COMETH

Tor Books by John Farris

JOHN FARRIS

THE AXMAN COMETH

A TOM DOHERTY ASSOCIATES BOOK
NEW YORK

THE AXMAN COMETH

Copyright © 1989 by John Farris

A TOR Book
Published by Tom Doherty Associates, Inc.
49 West 24 Street
New York, NY 10010

ISBN: 0-812-50008-3   Can. ISBN: 0-812-50009-1

First edition: July 1989

Printed in the United States of America

0 9 8 7 6 5 4 3 2 1

To the Reader
From the Author

Because we are about to enter into a partnership for at least the length of time it takes you to read, and perhaps reread *The Axman Cometh*, I think we should be fair with each other.

I am not going to be easy on you. This is not a novel to nibble away at between planes or in that half hour you set aside before dinner to get some reading done. It is not a few comfortable goosebumps and then turn the corner of the page down and off to dreamland. *The Axman Cometh* is not your conventionally designed novel, with standard chapter breaks. It was planned to be read as a long story, at one sitting.

Not up to it? Can't spare the time? I'm sorry to lose you, but I think it's someone else's book you want this time.

Am I being unfair, Reader?

No. Because if you're willing to meet me exactly halfway, I'll deliver. It's my belief that you've never read anything like *The Axman Cometh*. I doubt that you will ever forget it. Give me the time. Settle down in your favorite chair, turn the TV off, take the phone off the hook. And I'll take you for a ride that will beat anything you've ever been on at Six Flags or Magic Mountain.

But let me warn you: once you're aboard, you won't be able to jump off. You're mine. And I'm not letting you go.

Okay, Reader?

I'm ready when you are. Just turn the page—

THE
AXMAN
COMETH

What scares you?

You mean here? New York? Highs. Lows. Penthouse terraces on the East Side. Then the subway, almost any subway station. Stenchy, screechy, overpoweringly stuffy in the summer. Damp, freezing in the winter. And I, I'm afraid of most of the people who ride the subways, people who aren't like me. Blacks, Asians, Puerto Ricans. I'm from Kansas, and I can't get used to them. Sorry, I just can't. I'm thirty-six years old and I've lived in New York for—is it twelve years now?—and I—back home (that's Emerson, Emerson, Kansas, population thirty thousand, it's almost right in the middle of the state, I'm sure you've heard of—) in Emerson there were like four black kids in high school, maybe ten families in town, and they were, they were just like the rest of us, none of us ever paid attention to their color—oh, God, OH SHIT, damn it, who am I TALKING to? Who are you? Do you have a face, do you have a name? Tell me who you are! Come out of the dark, show me your fucking face!

Don't get excited. We've met before.

"Help me, please! Can anyone *hear* me? It's Shannon, Shannon Hill! I'm stuck here, I'm in the elevator! Could somebody please call the fire department!!"

It won't help if you let yourself panic. Don't lose control. If you lose control, then you'll lose me.

Shut up shut up shut up! I don't care! Who you are! Where you are! Why don't you help me get out of here . . .

*I hurt my hand. I mean, it really hurts! I shouldn't have hit the door like that. I always did such dumb things when I was a kid, have these tantrums and wind up hurting myself— but why don't they hear me? There's got to be somebody left in this building! Petra's still up- stairs, she must be, she said she had to work late. But if the power's off—I wish I could see. Something. Anything. It's so **dark.***

*You're not saying anything. But I know what you're thinking. I'm not afraid of the dark. Not that much. It's the elevator. I have **never*** *liked elevators. I always knew this was going to happen, I'd get stuck on one. By myself. All by mys—*

You're not alone.

Like hell I'm not! That's **BULLSHIT,** *I am alone, and I'm not crazy either!*

Of course you're not crazy.

"Then why am I talking to you? Why can you hear me? Who *are* you, you son of a bitch?"

Huh? Can't answer that, can you?

Can *you*, Shannon?

"I heard that! You *are* here! Right inside here with me! How . . . how did you . . . get on this elevator, I never saw—"

Stop it, Shannon; you're hyperventilating. You'll black out. Cup your hands over your face. Breathe into your hands. Slide down the wall until you're sitting on the floor. No, don't scream. Don't. We may be here for a long time. These old buildings, nothing works right. But the elevator's okay. It was built to carry big, heavy loads. It won't fall. You're not going to fall, Shannon.

"Ohh—kayy."

Now you have to try to get control of yourself. For your sake. For **mine.**

"Muuu — therrrrrr!"

That's right, Shannon. Go to mother. Talk to her. And you'll feel better.

*My   muutherrrrr   ss   **deadddd**   !*

Is she, Shannon?
Try real hard now, and I promise you'll see her—that's her, isn't it? In the back

4

yard, wearing those old yellow pedal pushers and her floppy gardening hat, hoeing the bean rows near the fence. Talking to Mrs. Mayhew while she works. You see her there, Mrs. Mayhew? How did your father describe her? "Ugly as a tattooed lip." The old sailor man had a way with words, didn't he?

The old—? Ohhhhh Jesus, now I know who you are, you're—

No. He died. You found that out, didn't you? Don't think about sad things. Just think about your mother for now. Speak to her, Shannon.

(So mild a day, she might be dreaming it. Yet the feel of deep spring grass on her bare feet and ankles is as real, as thrilling as the first kiss from the first boy she ever cared about. Shannon is four months from her seventeenth birthday. It is a Saturday in mid-May in Emerson, Kansas, 1964. There are twenty-two days until the Axman cometh.)

"Mom! Hi, Mrs. Mayhew."

Madge Mayhew, triple-chinned and with fool's gold hair, winds up an anecdote about hijinks at the most recent convocation of the Order of the Eastern Star, of which she is a past Matron, and both women smile at her.

"Hello, darlin'," Mayhew says. "What have you got there?"

"Oh, just some drawings I made," Shannon says secretively, holding the pad under her right arm. Her lower lip is tinted from the watercolor pens she habitually moistens with her tongue: a blue streak here, red there, so that she looks partially made up for a tribal celebration.

Ernestine Hill straightens from the chore of mulching between butterbean poles in her sixth of an acre of garden, the light coming into her face as her hat brim lifts, illuminating freckles that reappear with the warm weather like wildflowers, the wide calm gray eyes and unplucked brows, the nub of a hand-rolled cigarette poised on a flaky underlip.

Shannon says to Ernestine, in a significantly lower voice that Mrs. Mayhew, who has the ears of a wild hare, is still going to overhear with ease, "Do you think I should say anything . . . ?"

Ernestine strips one of her brown cotton work gloves (thirty-nine cents a pair at Dab's Hardware), and with the free hand takes a drag on what's left of her cigarette. Turns and squints at her neighbor, who has the sun behind her, and says with a smile, "I don't know why not. If you're going to pull this thing off, you'll need Madge's help too."

"Now what are you two cooking up?" Madge Mayhew says with conspiratorial glee, leaning her two hundred pounds against the post-and-wire fence where it's shakiest.

Ernestine limps out of her bean patch to have a sip of sweet tea from her jug. Severely malnourished during her formative years in the dustbowl thirties, she has poor bones, chronic back problems that require her to wear a brace, the knees of a dinosaur. Yet she is obsessive about gardening, her only recreation. Unlike Mrs. Mayhew, she belongs to no clubs and gently sneers at "all that joinin'."

"I guess you know Dab's coming up on fifty," Ernestine says.

"It *is* next month, isn't it? I always do get Dabney's birthday mixed up with my step-brother Horace's. One's the fifth of June and the other's the seventh, but for the life of me—"

"It'll be the fifth—"

"And we're going to give him the surprise of his life!" Shannon exclaims, beckoning for the jug of tea with which her mother has just refreshed herself. But Ernestine refuses to share, with a shake of her head and a little lift of the shoulders as if to indicate the jug is now empty. Or else she doesn't want Shannon to taste what she's cut the tea with.

"A *surprise* party! Oh, listen, you can count on me—this goes *no* farther! Who all are you going to invite?"

"I don't know," Ernestine says, lowering herself to the arm of a wooden lawn chair that Shannon sees, with a critical eye, needs repainting before the party. "Shannon's the one who thought of this. She's making all the arrangements."

Shannon nods, an emphatic affirmation of the magnitude of her plans.

"I'm sending out a hundred and fifty invitations—mom, do you think there's any chance Uncle Gilmore would come?"

"I couldn't say." Ernestine blows smoke, showing the underside of her upper lip like a whinnying horse. "It's a long way from Miles City, Montana. Plus the fact that Gil was never your father's favorite brother. And vice-versa. That Gilmore will offer to jack your jaw over the *pettiest* of things."

"Well, but he's the only brother Dab has

left, and this is an important occasion."

"Did I ever tell you Gil got drunk at our wedding and tried to—no, I never did tell you kids things like that."

"Tell her later," Madge says, "and me too if it's one I didn't hear already. I've always deeply regretted that you don't have a picture of him wearing the bridal bouquet like a— well, I just don't know how to say it politely."

"Jockstrap," Shannon says, affecting boredom, "I've been hearing all about it since I was ten."

Ernestine chuckles, throwing away the little bit remaining of her cigarette as Madge returns her attention to Shannon and the surprise party.

"A hundred and fifty people! Where are you going to find a place in the neighborhood with enough room, except maybe the Sunday school building or the VFW."

"Right here. Our back yard's plenty big enough! I'm going to decorate—you know, with Japanese lanterns and stuff."

"That's a *nice* idea. I could give you a hand with the food."

"Would you, Mrs. Mayhew?"

"Sure, we'll keep everything in our garage, in washtubs and that spare Frigidaire Adolphus got to running again the other day. Otherwise, how're you going to keep it a secret from Dab? What about entertainment

—you know, if you play your cards right, Adolphus could probably persuade the Old Warhorses to do their act. Costumes and all." The Old Warhorses are a barbershop quartet; Madge Mayhew's husband is the somewhat creaky baritone of the cornball group. Most everybody in town calls him "Ragtop" because of the quality of his ill-fitting hairpiece.

Shannon says cautiously, "Oh, thanks, Mrs. Mayhew, but—I think I've got a band already, some guys I know from the college."

"Do they play rot-and-roll?" Madge says, accusingly, then relents in her condemnation. "Well, I suppose all the young people will want that caterwauling. Anyway, I think this party of yours is going to be a peck of fun!"

Shannon glances at her mother, who nods but with no show of approval, then gets up to hobble over to the quart cans of tomato plants she is planning to set out when she finishes with the beans.

"The only thing to watch out for," cautions Ernestine, "is the weather. Better check your *Old Farmers*. Because there's no way we're going to try to fit one-hundred-fifty people in *my* house. Provided that many trouble to show up. By the way, where are they all going to park?"

"Church lot. It's only a couple of blocks." Shannon, convinced of her mother's lack of enthusiasm, uncovers the sketch pad and moves closer to the fence to show her work to her new ally Mrs. Mayhew.

"Here's how I'm going to do the invitations."

"Well, look there! Did you draw that? Isn't that Popeye the sailorman?"

"It'll look more like Dab when I'm finished."

"And there's you and Chap and Allen Ray in sailor suits! And Ernestine too! Why, these pitchers are just as clever as they can be! What d'you call 'em, caricatures? Like some of those editorial cartoons in the Topeka *Capital* that get Adolphus so riled he could spit bloody gallstones. Ernestine, you have just got to come look at this!"

Ernestine obligingly leaves her tomato plants and, over Shannon's shoulder, studies the caricatures on the sketch pad.

" 'Ain't it nifty? Dab is fifty.' Well, now. That's very clever, Shannon."

"This girl has *talent* to spare. Nobody can tell me any different."

"I'm going to write and illustrate my own books," Shannon mumbles, flushed and happy. "I've got some ideas already."

"She's just full of ideas," Ernestine agrees, but with that faint tone of belittlement Shannon thinks she hears lately; wondering if it somehow has to do with her mother growing older in pain, limiting herself more and more to house and garden while Shannon dreams, aloud, of the wide world, of accomplishment and fame. "Have you given any thought as to how much this party will cost?"

"Yes," Shannon says. "Three hundred fifty dollars for everything, that's food and drinks too. We're all going to share the cost—I mean, I'll pay a hundred, Allen Ray says he'll give me another hundred and Chap is good for fifty, he's saved more than that from his paper route. Then, I thought you might—"

"Sure, count me in for fifty," Ernestine says, smiling, her little teeth like ruined corn in a parched field. She pulls on her shabby work glove. "It'll be worth it, just to see the expression on Dab's face. But you never know which way his mood's going to go, Shannon. He may get the sulks and ruin the party for everybody."

Shannon experiences a sudden hostile closing of her throat, swallows, waits three sharp heartbeats and then is compelled to say, swiftly and cruelly, "You don't want to do this, do you? If it wasn't for me, you wouldn't do anything—oh, bake another cake. Same as always."

Ernestine looks at her, unruffled but with the bleakness of one who has successfully throttled all temperament, and says, "You have to understand how Dab and me feel about things—as we get on in life."

"I think he's going to have a perfectly wonderful time! Because—all we ever do is take Dab for granted; when has anyone ever treated him as if he was important?"

"Well, that's the way it is, isn't it?" Ernestine says, casting around ironically, taking in the neighborhood, all of the small city in which they live. "When you come down to it, who matters that much?"

"Dab's important to me!"

"Okay, then," Ernestine says, with her air of edgy agreeableness, "coming from you, this party'll mean something to him. Like as not."

Madge says, re-tuning the conversation as if it were a static-y radio, "How are you going to keep the party a secret from Dab? If you plan to string up Japanese lanterns and all—"

"Oh, we can do that the day of the party. Dab always closes up at six-thirty, but on Friday nights he usually takes an hour after work to go over accounts at the back of the store. He won't get home until it's almost dark."

"That'll work," Madge says, nodding. "I'll have to tell Adolphus that something's afoot, but you know how he is, Shannon:

13

never says two words to anybody unless it's politics. Then you can't shut him up."

Ernestine pulls a little sack of cigarette tobacco from a pocket of the Navy surplus shirt she wears to garden. She cocks an ear.

"Washing machine's on spin, and it's out of balance. Can you get those clothes on the line while we've got this nice breeze?"

Shannon sprints across the deep yard to the back porch. "I'm going to give Uncle Gilmore a call!"

"Wait til after five o'clock!" Ernestine advises. "No sense running up our phone bill over a lost cause!"

Shannon's older brother Allen Ray is a late riser. In pajama bottoms and a fading, sunflower yellow-and-brown high-school athletic jersey he stands in front of the open refrigerator in the kitchen drinking milk from a bottle. "This milk's old," he complains. He finishes it anyway. Allen Ray is nineteen. He works at the T & P Garage and races his stock car on five-eighths of a mile oval dirt tracks around Emerson and as far north as Nebraska. His draft board has called him for his physical the second week in June, and Shannon is worried, with Vietnam an increasingly prominent topic on the nightly television news. He comes out to the porch with a doughnut and watches Shannon reorder the load of wet wash in the drum of their old

Bendix. "What's a lost cause?"

"Uncle Gilmore. Mom doesn't think he'll come. Look at the drawings I did for the invitations."

"Oh. Neat."

"How did you make out last night in Ellsworth?"

"Blew a head. Finished fourth."

"How much was that worth?"

"Twenty-five bucks."

"Do you think they'll take you?"

"What? Oh, the Army. Sure, they'll take me. I'm a perfect physical specimen." Allen Ray, habitually slouchy, straightens and flexes his biceps. The fly front of his pajamas gaps open.

"So I see," Shannon says with a smirk. Allen Ray grins and turns away to close up. "Allen Ray?"

"Yo."

"Why don't you join the Navy first, before you're drafted? That'd make Dab so proud."

"Boats," Allen Ray says disdainfully. "I'm going to be a tanker."

"Like Elvis?"

Allen Ray licks cinnamon and sugar from his fingers. "I think that was all publicity. I'll bet they never let him anywhere *near* a tank."

Shannon begins singing "Return to

Sender" in a small but true voice and turns the washing machine on again. It doesn't sound right, and her brother is frowning. "What do you think's the matter, Allen Ray?"

"Bearing."

"Can you fix it?"

"Tomorrow. I'm late for work."

"Oh, would you drop me by school?"

"Saturday? What's going on?"

"Prom committee, then I've got to get ready for the art exhibit in the library."

"Who's taking you to the prom?"

"Three guesses, first two don't count."

"Most Likely to Succeed. At what?"

"At using his head. Full scholarship to Washburn. Are you going to marry Sondra before you get drafted?"

"Hell no. What is she going to do, follow me around from Texas to Germany?"

"She could live here with us," Shannon says as the idea pops into her head. "I like Sondra. It'd be great to have somebody almost my own age to talk to."

"I'm not getting married so you'll have somebody to talk to," Allen Ray replies with that sardonic little twist of the lip that is, to a T, his mother. Shannon mimics him and Allen Ray turns with a shrug. "Look, I'm going to pull on some clothes and go. You ready, or what?"

16

"Right with you. I just need to get this load of sheets on the line—"

"They're pretty bloody, aren't they?" Allen Ray says. But so is he. Shannon looks up from pulling the stained, dripping sheets out of the Bendix to see him hanging by one arm caught in pincers of broken glass in the kitchen door, his throat —open— almost to
the back of his neck,
showing the severed ends
of the tough, bone-white
windpipe.

    Even

before she begins to shriek,
the dark returns: it's very, very

    dark

there on West Homestead in
Emerson, Kansas; up and down
the familiar street where the
typical night sounds are from dogs,
insects, television (the
Rockweilers have a new RCA color

console that set them back seven hundred
ninety five dollars;
it's the first one on the
block), the rumblings of dual
carbs on Duffy Satterstall's '57
Chevy while he endlessly tunes
the spotless engine, and
bicycle

bells

as the McMicken twins head home
from a Little League game
on the diamond behind First Pres,
quarreling, as they are
apt to do, over which of them
made the best or worst plays . . .

but nobody, nobody
has ever thoroughly shattered
the peace of West Homestead
Avenue with scream

after

scream of bloody murder, until

18

SIX DEAD
IN EMERSON
MASSACRE

(The *Wichita Eagle*, June 9, 1964)

"I like to chop."

(Identical message found on the walls of four houses in Briarwood, Missouri, Crestview, Iowa, Hendricks, Nebraska, and Emerson, Kansas. September 1962 to June 1964.)

My Goddddd they're allllll deadddddd

Shannon. Shannon. Don't scream.

"I'm going to die! I've got to get out of here, this fucking elevator: somebody, **somebody** please hear me!!"

I hear you. I'm with you. I'm listening.

"But you don't **do** anything! You're not helping me! I'm choking, I can't breathe! Get Don. Please get Don for me, he'll know what to do, he'll get me out of here!"

Donald Carnes?

"Yes! Who do you think I'm talking— but you don't know him. How could you know Don?"

You let him down, Shannon. Called the wedding off. That was five months ago. I'm afraid you won't be seeing—

"I know we haven't **seen** each other, but we've talked—I tried to explain to him why—why I couldn't—but I still love him! He knows that! We're having a drink together, tonight—at Cabrera's on Columbus. Where we met. Oh, God. How long have I been trapped in here? I must be late already. What is Don going to think?"

But he doesn't mean anything to you anymore. I'm the one who matters to you, Shannon. I'm the only one who's ever mattered.

"You're a liar! You don't know me! God, if it wasn't so dark in here—"

But it's the dark that has brought us together. And when you want to see me, you will.

Noooo . . . no. Don—Donald! For the love of God, come! Find me. Before it's too late!

"Having another, Mr. Carnes?"

(Cabrera's. 385 Columbus Avenue, between 78th and 79th. The food is Cuban. The bar is on your right as you go in, and it's a big bar, popular in the neighborhood. Salsa on the quad speakers, Miami Sound Machine. Fresh, lightly salted *tostones* in wicker baskets spaced along the mahogany bar. *Calamares* to order with Cabrera's special sauce. These go very well with another house specialty, double frozen daiquiris without sugar, "Papa *dobles*," made just the way the great author himself used to drink them at the Floridita Bar. It is unclear if the owner or owners of Cabrera's knew the Nobel laureate, or if he ever graced their New York restaurant, but behind the bar amid other celebrity photos is one of Hemingway, impressively rotund and

23

shaggy in slacks and a *guayabera*, standing on the veranda of the *Finca Vigilia* on the island, holding a cat in the crook of one arm, "Black Dog" at his heel. Papa's expression is beclouded, unsmiling, as he faces down the perhaps barely tolerated photographer.

On a rainy Tuesday night in October, with a radical change of weather in the offing, there are only half a dozen regulars at Cabrera's bar. Along with Donald B. (for Burnside) Carnes, who used to be a semiregular, when he lived nearby at Amsterdam and 72nd. Don is thirty-six. His income is sixty-two thousand a year, and he's in his thirteenth year with New York Life. Actuarial, not Sales. He has a secure position in a branch of his depression-proof business, where there is usually a shortage of capable men and women.

Don Carnes turns on his stool to look at the doorway through which no one has come for the last ten minutes, then at the coatroom girl with the dark flowing hair that hides part of her comely, caramel face but not the vivid plump mouth that invites lolling, like a waterbed. She is listlessly turning over the pages of the *New York Post*, looks up to find his eyes on her and smiles, giving her head and mane a little shake as if to exhibit sympathy, realizing that he is waiting for someone now long past due; but Don looks like a man who has known his share of frustration, waiting for blind dates in neighborhood watering holes. He's a little plump and a little short. From his father he inherited male pattern baldness, and from his mother a poor pair of eyes (astigmatism). Yet there's something about Don that invites confidences, when you get to know him. Stability. The staunch in him implicit, like the ribs of a whaling vessel. There are people who like listening to other people, and those, the majority, who are just waiting for their turn to talk. Don is a listener. One night shortly after she met him at a party (they weren't even dating), Shannon stopped making small talk, looked, for about twenty suspenseful and silent seconds, into his serious brown eyes, then began pouring out her heart. Before the evening was over she knew she was in love. Unfortunately for Shannon—

"Mr. Carnes?"

"Oh, sorry, Francisco, I didn't mean to be rude." Don looks at his empty glass, looks at his watch, a square, sensible Timex he bought for $12.95 more than eight years ago. *Takes a licking, keeps on ticking*, as John Cameron Swayze used to say.

The bartender is about five feet tall, dark and dry as an unwrapped mummy, with a nap of terrycloth-white hair. Everybody else calls him "Frank," but Don adheres to a certain formality in his dealings with people he hasn't known all of his life.

25

"Your lady," Francisco says, "is running late tonight?"

"She sure is. Forty minutes late. She had a five-thirty meeting with her editor, I think. And the publishing house is pretty far downtown, almost in the Village."

"Ah, the one who writes and illustrates children's books. I have forgotten her name."

"Shannon," Don says, the sound of it unexpectedly sweet to his ears. For a couple of moments his lower lip is unsteady, like a child's.

"We have not seen either of you here for many months, ¿verdad?"

"Yes, well, we—broke off. This is the first time—"

The front door opens to laughter, a gust of chill wet air, the distant electronic blurt of police sirens, and Don turns quickly; but it's three Latins, two men in silk suits with rain in their hair, a woman carrying a raffish miniature poodle wearing a rhinestone choker. Don turns around again and catches sight of himself in the backbar glass looking uncharacteristically disgruntled as he thinks, *Why did I let her talk me into this? It's no good for either one of us.*

"Here you are, sir."

"Thanks, Francisco."

Don glances at the telephone at one end of the bar and wonders if it's worth trying to find out if she's actually coming, maybe just stuck in traffic is all—if her conference with the editor, Petra what's-her-name, was running overtime, then Shannon, flighty and neurotic but never discourteous, would surely give him a jingle after going to so much trouble to set them up for the evening. Maybe worth spending a quarter just to make sure she'd already left.

"I remember some of the *fantastico* pictures she drew. Such strange creatures, enough to frighten small children, I should think."

You ought to see the ones nobody in their right minds would publish in books for children, Don says to himself. *I didn't like looking at them either.* But maybe getting those drawings out of her system had been as effective as several more years of psychotherapy.

Don puts one foot on the floor (black Peal shoes, the best, and expensive, but made for a lifetime: one superlative pair of shoes, or twenty pairs of Florsheims that lose their shape in a hard rain? Penny-wise or pound-foolish. He is a man who knows the true value of everything he purchases, or contemplates purchasing some day), fishes for a quarter in the coin pocket of his dark blue suit pants (Brooks Brothers. Always correct, never out of style).

"Believe I'll just call and see what the

delay is," Don says to Francisco, as if he owes the Cuban an explanation for continuing to hang around his bar.

He carries his daiquiri with him and puts it on the sill beneath the telephone after another long sip (the glass only half empty but already he anticipates ordering another; he's feeling a touch reckless as well as disgruntled —might as well go ahead and get well-fortified for what's coming when Shannon arrives; tomorrow he's working at home where he can nurse a hangover privately). From another pocket he takes a thin, credit-card-size calculator that also stores up to two hundred telephone numbers and addresses and recalls the number for Knightsbridge Publishers.

Ten minutes past eight. The phone is ringing, but he is already convinced it won't be answered. So what to do? Sit in the bar and drink frozen daiquiris until it's certain that Shannon has stood him up? Don knows she is not capable of deliberately humiliating him; no, his humiliation lies in his need to see her once more, knowing full well that they—

"Hello?"

"Oh—hello. I—who's this?"

"Who's calling?" she replies, a little curt with him.

"Is this the office of Knightsbridge Publishers?"

"Yes, it is."

"Well, I was wondering, you have an editor there named Petra; I'm sorry, I can't recall—"

"This is Petra Kisber speaking."

"My name is Donald Carnes. I believe we've met."

"Oh, *yes*, you're—"

"—a friend of Shannon Hill's. Is she still there? We had a—an appointment, but—"

"No, Shannon left some time ago. As the Fates would have it, I seem to be the only one who's stuck up here."

"Stuck?"

"On the top floor. There's no power. It's the whole neighborhood again, from what I can tell. That's three outages, as ConEd quaintly calls them, in the past eight months. It's really a disgrace. But I was ready for this one. I bought a pair of old hurricane lamps in Port Antonio this summer, thank God, and kept one here at the office just in case."

"That is fortunate. I assume the elevator isn't operating?"

"Ha! It doesn't run half the time when there *is* power. I hate and despise the damned thing, it's as big as a cattle car and *sooo* slow. And it never hits the floor exactly even; you have to step up eight inches, or down six inches—"

"You can't use the stairs to—"

"In this building? *This* neighborhood? It was a department store a hundred years ago, but the building went to pot after World War Two. A few years ago somebody got the bright idea of restoring the facade, which I have to admit is quite elegant, and converting several floors inside to office space. But they ran out of money, so the first couple of floors are deserted except for derelicts and God knows who else—walk? This far downtown, with the lights out? Not Petra Kisber. I'm perfectly happy to sit here with the doors locked, and I just *hope* the paraffin in this lamp doesn't give out . . . hmm, what was that?"

"Excuse me?"

"I thought I heard something just now. Someone scr—yelling. No, it must have been outside on the street."

"Miss Kisber—"

"Just call me Petra. I'm now managing editor, by the way. Excalibur Books."

"Yes, I've seen some of them. Very impressive. I wonder if—how long after Shannon left your office did the power fail?"

"I'm not sure. Let's see. I didn't walk her out, as I usually do—frankly, I had to use the little girl's sandbox, so that's where I was, sitting on the john when the lights went off. I'm telling you, I just about wrecked my shins getting back to my office—in the dark this floor is a maze of partitions and bookshelves. And wastebaskets: people will leave their wastebaskets anywhere. I'm writing a memo about that first thing in the—"

"There's a possibility that Shannon and perhaps others could be in the elevator, between floors?"

"Nobody else from here. I was the last one in the office. The floor below is vacant. And I doubt if the night cleaning crew shows up much before midnight."

"Is there an emergency alarm to ring?"

"Not in the elevator. Like I said, it's an old freight job with these massive gates Superman couldn't open by himself."

"Would you mind going to find out if anyone's trapped?"

"The elevator's clear on the other side of the building, and I don't mind admitting I'm getting a little stressed out being here all by my lonesome. I'd just as soon stay—"

Don pauses to drain the rest of his daiquiri, and, in the lifting of his arm, is aware that his armpits are icy, he is feeling more than a little apprehensive.

"Petra, if, just possibly, Shannon's in that elevator—by herself—imagine how *she* must feel."

"Weren't you two going to get married? I got the invitation and bought the most elegant

—then wasn't it about three days before the wedding—?"

Don has long ago become sick of hearing about wedding gifts that had to be returned. "It's a long story. Listen to me, now. You don't know Shannon as well as I do—no one does. It would—be very bad for her to be by herself in that elevator. There could be serious psychological consequences."

"You mean she's claustrophobic?"

"Oh, I mean much worse than that." And he feels the sliding of icy sweat beads down his right side beneath his shirt.

"Hmm. Then I suppose I should—but I don't think there's a thing I can do if she's actually trapped—"

"The fire department will deal with that situation."

"I could stay here and call them. But if she's not in the elevator, then it's like turning in a false alarm, isn't it?"

"Petra. Please. Go find out if Shannon is in that elevator!"

"You're right. I ought to do that. I can put myself in her shoes. I'd certainly want somebody to come looking for me."

"Call me back. I'm at Cabrera's, on Columbus Avenue. The number is—"

Don reads it off for her, solicits further assurances that Petra will proceed to the elevator to find out if it is occupied, then notify the fire department. And call him. He hangs up and goes back to his seat at the bar with his empty glass; as soon as he sits down Francisco slides a fresh "Papa *doble*" toward him. In the photograph on the back bar old Hemingway looks testier than ever, probably wishing somebody would fix him a frosty strengthener.

"I heard," Francisco says. "I hope your lady is not in the elevator after all."

"Oh, God," Don says dismally, wiping his brow with a cocktail napkin, "you and me both, Frank."

Draw me.

I'm so thirsty! I wish I had something to drink. What I'd like right now is a draft beer— no, better than that, one of Cabrera's huge frozen daiquiris, in a goddamn beer mug. I'd give anything for—what did you say?

I want you to draw me, Shannon.

"Are you crazy? We're in the dark—I don't even know where you are." *I'm not sure you—*

Exist?

*That's what I was afraid of! I'm talking to myself! I **am** losing my mind!*

No, you're not.

"Then—prove it to me. I'm here. I can't go anywhere, so—reach out and—and touch me."

I'd like to, Shannon. But I can't. First you have to draw me. The dark doesn't matter. You have your sketch pad with you. Your drawing pencils. Do me in charcoal. Your brain knows. Your hand will know. Draw me.

But if I do that—

What, Shannon?

No, I can't. I won't do it—I've never been able to do it!

If you let me out, then I'll let you out. You've always wanted to know the truth, Shannon. You've always wanted to be sure. Now is the time.

"I don't trust you! Stay where you belong, you son of a bitch—! Ah. Ahhh, ahhhhh!"

If you let yourself get hysterical, you won't be able to breathe. You could die here, Shannon, before anyone finds you. Die of suffocation in this elevator. We don't want that to happen. So get busy. Open your case. Take out your pencils. And draw me.

("Draw Me." On a plain piece of white paper, no more than eight-and-a-half-by-eleven inches. Sometimes it was a girl in the ads, sometimes the head of a dog in profile, done with economical charcoal strokes. When she was eleven Shannon had copied one of the drawings that appealed to her, a Dalmatian, and mailed it for a free evaluation of her potential. Unsurprisingly she was informed by the art school that she would be squandering a valuable talent if she didn't immediately sign up for the home-study course they offered. There was a convenient monthly payment plan. Shannon loved to draw but she didn't like to "study," so she continued to learn in her own way, by trial and error, winning school competitions every year through eleventh grade for her pastels and watercolors.)

"What's that going to be?" Chapman Hill asks his sister, who is hard at work on the back porch where the light is stronger after school than in her room.

"What does it look like?"

"Just a barn. Ho hum. Who needs another picture of an old barn?"

"It's not the object, it's how the artist perceives it," Shannon says with a slight frown, not looking up from her wide brush strokes.

"Huh?"

"Never mind. Don't you have anything to do but hang around the house?" Like a mother, nagging; in a way Shannon, five years older than her brother, is more of a mother to Chap than Ernestine. Who is fond of saying, *I never expected to have more than two*, and treats the boy with what amounts to indifference, as if he is a neighbor's child temporarily misplaced. "And don't get any closer with that fudgecicle, you're dripping."

There's a streak of chocolate down his bare chest, to his navel. Chap is wearing only a pair of raggedy shorts, and he's nearly as tan as he will get all summer. He already has his summer haircut, although there are two more weeks of school left, and his ears stick out woefully. Chap is the only one of the three children to get his father's ears, for which Shannon is grateful: ears don't make any difference to boys.

"You're dripping too."

"On purpose; that's my *technique*, it's part of the painting."

"No, I mean you got a spot of black paint there on your red paint."

Shannon moistens the tip of a little finger with her tongue and wipes away the spot from the scarlet oval in her twenty-four-color tray. The telephone rings. "Grab that; mom's lying down with a headache."

"Ho hum. Are you sure it's a headache she's got?"

"What's that supposed to mean, of course I'm sure! Answer the G.D. phone, *Chap*man!"

"Found another empty bottle of vodka in the garbage. That makes two this week."

"What were you doing in the garbage?"

"I always look in the garbage," Chapman replies, sauntering into the kitchen. "I like to see what we're throwing out. All I'm trying to tell you is, she's at it again—hello? What? No, sir, I'm Chap, Allen Ray's at work. Who's this? You are? We did? I dunno. You want to talk to my sister?"

"Who is it?"

Chap appears in the doorway with the receiver of the telephone stretched to its limit on a long cord. "Say's he's Uncle Gilmore."

"Oh, give me the phone quick! Jesus, Chapman, you got chocolate all over—hello? Uncle Gilmore, it's Shannon! Yes, I did call you—oh, everything's all right . . . hope I didn't give you *that* idea. He's just fine. How about yourself?"

Shannon leans against the jamb of the door to the kitchen, cringing as Chapman gives her a "chocolate hickey" on the neck before springing outside in response to a call from Aaron Wurzheimer, three doors down, his best friend even though the Wurzheimers are Lutherans and the families don't socialize. Shannon pictures Uncle Gilmore as she drew him nearly three years ago, when he dropped by the house for a few hours' visit following an Elks' convention in Kansas City: a runt of a countryman with stubble, florid and bald; he had hooded licorice eyes and a turned-down mouth that could snap shut with surprising ferocity.

"You probably know," she says, when Gilmore runs out of bad things to say about the winter he's been through and the small rancher's plight at the hands of Eastern Liberal Democrats, and never mind where Lyndon

Johnson hails from, "that it's Dab's fiftieth birthday coming up—no, the fifth of June—and we're having this big surprise party for him; everybody's coming. So I was kind of hoping you could be here too."

"Well, gal, I just don't know. Spring is my busiest time, with so many heavies to look after. I did need to make a trip down to Whichertaw along about in June, so I suppose there is a chance—"

"We'd love to see you. What's a 'heavy?' "

"Heifer with calf. 'Preciate you thinkin' about me, though. You'd be, what, about seventeen now?"

"In four months. Will you try real hard to make it?"

"Can't promise much; but thanky for the invitation. Got to git now."

"Give my best to Aunt Zelma and cousin Auline—" Shannon says hurriedly, hearing her uncle call to another part of his house just before hanging up, "Naw, it ain't that, Zelma, it's just some goddamn birthday part—"

Wincing, Shannon feels eyes on her and glances over her shoulder at the screen door of the back porch; she almost drops the receiver of the telephone because somebody is standing there, on the top step, looking in at her; nobody she can recognize because the sun is behind him.

"Hi."

"Who is it?"

"Oh, it's me—Perry. Perry Kennold. From school."

"Yeah? Hi. What are you—excuse me, I need to hang up the phone. Did you want to come in or something?"

"Just wondered if I could get a drink of water. I was out walking, but I don't know anybody on this street. Except you. Didn't you used to have a dog? I was kind of afraid I'd run into your dog, but nobody answered the front door."

"Borneo. He got leukemia and we had to put him away last month. We were all sick about it. Come on in, I'll just—water's okay? We've got ginger ale and Dr Pepper."

"Maybe a Dr Pepper if that wouldn't be too much trouble."

"No, have a seat. Perry. Be right back. How did you know we had a dog?"

"Oh, I was this way before. On your street."

"Where do you live?" Shannon asks him, opening the refrigerator. One interruption after another, she really wanted to get some painting done. She takes out a couple of bottles of Dr Pepper. And now it's almost time to think about supper. Dab and Allen Ray both get home a little past six-thirty, and they can be difficult to put up with if supper's not piping hot and on the table the minute they hit the door. Shannon knows Ernestine won't be down for the rest of the day. Not when she's in one of her prize moods. Shannon doesn't want to think about the empty bottles of vodka, but she has no reason to doubt Chap's word. He has always kept an observant eye on his mother, not out of malice but as if she is some sort of long-term nature-study project he has adopted.

"I live at the trailer park."

She might have guessed. There's only one in town, and not a very inviting place to live, filled with the sort of people who drive unwashed pickup trucks, have common-law spouses and get into knife fights.

"I didn't know that." She knows nothing about Perry Kennold. He's a recent transfer student, junior, sits in her fourth-period biology class. *Sits* is about all. He seems never to open his mouth or his textbook, but she has observed him surreptitiously reading a paperback edition of Walt Whitman with a kind of avid, worshipful look in his eyes.

Shannon carries the Dr Peppers out to the porch, grateful for a breeze that has come up as the sun sinks just below the high crowns of sage orange and persimmon trees in the backyard.

Perry is looking at her latest watercolor.

"I saw some of your other pictures in the library," he says. "You're real good. I'd like to be able to draw."

"Do you take art?"

"No. I wouldn't be any good at it. I don't have any talent."

He looks up at her as she hands him the Dr Pepper. His hand overlaps hers for just a moment, unexpectedly clammy, she feels calluses. He's a real big kid, especially through the shoulders, but unfortunately he has acne, even on the back of his neck where his hair is longest but doesn't hide the lumps. His face is so nicked and scabby it looks as if he went through a windshield. Forget about the acne and he's really good-looking, with a Roman nose and thick, dark eyelashes. But then you notice he's minus a front tooth and always seems to be self-conscious about that, holding his head down when he talks, or shielding his mouth with one hand. He's a moody sort and Shannon is intolerant of people who can't find something to be glad about once in a while; but, perversely, there are depths to his moodiness that arouse her mothering instinct.

Because his acne makes it hard for her

to look him straight in the face, she goes to the screen with her own soda and stares out at the backyard. Behind the Hill house Madge Mayhew is taking wash off her line. Sheets flap briskly in the wind and Shannon thinks, creatively, of sailing ships: some day she will paint the sea in all its moods. The challenge in store gives her gooseflesh.

"So how come you're over here?" Shannon asks, not meaning anything particularly, but it comes out sounding like she thinks he is out of bounds and uninvited. Then, before Perry can answer, she gets that little alerting flash across the horizon of her mind: he's been around before, on West Homestead, he's here this afternoon because—Shannon remembers his first day at the high school, his eyes on her in biology, brooding but appreciative—Perry Kennold has a crush on her. How terrific.

"I don't know. I walk around a lot. Nothing else to do, if you know what I mean. I don't have a car."

"I always have more to do than I can find time for," Shannon says blithely, hoping he will take the hint. She glances at him, not smiling. He has taken a couple of sips of the Dr Pepper, not as if he is dying of thirst, and that cinches it: he just wanted an excuse to talk to her. Ho hum. He's wearing the same clothes he seems to wear every day to school. Unironed Levi's, a white T-shirt and denim vest with a fleece lining that's too warm for the season, rough-out boots so shabby the stitches appear barely to be holding.

"Do you think Oswald killed Kennedy? I don't."

The assassination was a personal tragedy for Shannon. She doesn't like being reminded of it, or discussing an idol with a virtual stranger.

"I don't know; I try not to think about it any more."

"Did you cry?" he asks softly.

Now that is going too far, and Shannon shrugs hostilely. Perry looks at the floor, has another sip of soda.

"Anybody else home?"

The question makes Shannon uneasy. "My mother's upstairs. Resting. My little brother's next door, and Allen Ray'll be along in a minute."

"He's the one who played football?"

"You know a lot about us," Shannon says, smiling tautly.

"I just happened to see his picture in the trophy case at school and I thought, wow, he looks a lot like Shannon, he must be—how come he doesn't play college ball anywhere?"

"Allen Ray just got tired of football. And,

45

to tell the truth, he didn't have the grades for college. Do you play? You're big enough."

"I know. I weighed two-fifteen this morning in the locker room before P-E. I do about three-hundred push-ups every day." He pushes hard with a forefinger, showing her that he can't make much of a dent in a well-rounded bicep. "The good news is I'll probably go out for the team next season. The bad news is I might not be here." Shannon does not ask why. He shrugs as if, silent, she is only trying to hide consternation. "We move around a lot. My father does construction work. Drives Cats. Road graders, bulldozers."

"Do you have any brothers or sisters?"

"I had—have a sister. She got married to an ironworker on the Yellowtail Dam site. That's in Montana, near the Little Big Horn. And my mother ran off when we were living in Tucumcari; she took up with an accountant from Buffalo, New York, who was out west for his health. So it's just me and my father now."

"Uh-huh. You can take that Dr Pepper with you if you want. I really should get supper started, so I don't have time to talk."

"Oh. Right." Perry gets up looking chastened. "Thanks. This really hit the spot. Is this a deposit bottle? Tell you what, I'll bring it to you in school tomorrow."

("No, keep it," Shannon said, visualizing

Perry Kennold passing her an empty Dr Pepper bottle in biology lab; the embarrassment—. She turned away as if she was afraid she was going to laugh, but her heart was beating almost savagely and that's when he reached over her shoulder and touched her—touched her cheek with a slit, bleeding finger and said:

"See how sharp it is? I like to chop."

Or *was* it Perry?)

Petra Kisber, managing editor of Excalibur Books, thinks she is not alone.

There are two ways off the sixth (and top) floor of the building at Sixth Avenue and Nineteenth Street in lower Manhattan. One is by elevator, which is not working; the other is by the stairwell, the steel door to which is marked by an *exit* light which, as exit lights must do, glows in the blackout. In defiance of a city ordinance this door is always locked, although most of the forty-six employees of the Knightsbridge Publishing Company have keys.

Petra thinks she is not alone. Worse, she is sure she smells pigs.

There have been mornings in the city since she came to stay, simmering summer mornings before the streets are washed, when the rancid effluvium has reminded her of the barnyard, of hog wallow and slops and the pigs that terrified her long before a couple of sows devoured a neighbor's toddler back home in West Virginia: but for the most part she has put her country raising well behind her. Studied in Europe. Taken a new name. Petra, not Patricia. Lost the slow-pitch, hillbilly accent and improved herself through sheer willpower: diet, Hatha Yoga, postgrad courses at the New School. She lightened her hair and acquired a soul mate. If she returned to her home state now, after an absence of more than twenty years, not even her closest relatives would recognize her without prompting. She is not, however, about to go back to Buck Creek, West Virginia, for any reason.

But she still smells pigs. And she is not alone.

Sometimes, although there is nothing that specific to focus on (pigs? It could be the smell of the trashy street below, stewing in the rain, an olfactory reminder of her increasingly desperate desire to be out of here, well on her way home to a wood fire in their rent-controlled apartment on West End, drinks with Barbara while they cuddle on the sinfully comfortable plush sofa they have recently sprung for at an estate sale in Bedford Hills), even trivial discomforts or inconveniences can magnify the little fears that lie in the subconscious for their moments to come alive, to screech and howl and demoralize the hardiest of souls. And she has been more than two hours by herself in the dark and draughty offices of the Knightsbridge Publishing Company. Thank God for her lamp. Standing in front of the elevator doors, which are steel and of the clamshell type, opening top and bottom instead of from side to side, Petra raises the lamp, light reflecting from the glossily painted brick wall (puce; somebody's idea of decorator chic), as she turns slowly for a look behind her—hears a grunting, snuffling sound—and the fear drains from the roots of her hair in a cold flood, down her backbone and through her bowels, which have been none too secure today; hits the knees with tidal force and weakens them; surges back to the level of her heart, drowning her lungs.

"*Who is that?*" But she knows already. *It's pigs.*

Petra turns back and strikes at steel with her fist.

"Is anybody there? Can you hear me?" When there is no reply she presses against the doors at the head-high seam, listening. The sound that eventually comes back to her is faint, as if from the depths of a well: a child's lugubrious weeping.

"Shan? Is that you? Hey, it's Petra! We're going to be all right, *cheri*, it's . . . it was a power failure. The lights could go back on any—Shannon? Talk to me?"

No words, only the heartbroken weeping, so faint Petra must strain to discern what she hears.

"You'll be fine. I forgot to tell you—"

Petra, panicky for Shannon's sake (but is it Shannon?), takes a couple of deep, gulping breaths that fail to pacify; and she nearly gags on the odor, pig shit and soured garbage, that has filled the floor like fumes from a dump fire.

"Don called. I'm going to call him back

now, and tell him you're okay, just a little scared. Me too. Then I'm going to get hold of the fire department, but no telling how long it'll take them—probably not more than half an hour. They'll get you out of there if the power's not on by then—*Shannon, would you answer me!*"

She can't bear, any more, the ceaseless, hopeless weeping: as if Shannon's mind has snapped, or she has, in her terror at being trapped, regressed to her childhood. Poor baby—but Petra has her own expanding terror to deal with. She wants to go back to her office, *now*. Slam the door. Shut out the abominable pig stench, even if she must soak a handkerchief in the brandy she keeps in a desk drawer. But even with her nose anesthetized, how can she not hear pigs rooting and squealing (all of the child eaten, all but his clothes and skull with its neat rows of baby teeth)?

First she must deal with her retreat, through the narrow avenues between offices —Accounting, then Editorial, a book-lined maze. She is trying to remember where the nearest fire alarm is located: nothing to it, no phone call required. *In emergency break glass pull down handle*. The problem is—

When Petra, holding her lantern high, catches sight of the square red alarm box with a handy little hammer dangling from a chain, she also sees a big brindle sow, weighing upward of two hundred and fifty pounds, standing in the aisle blocking her way.

"You can't do this! I'm Petra, not Patricia! I'm the managing editor! Get away from me, you putrid hunk of bacon! I know you're not real, you can't be real!"

The sow grunts, lifting its pink snout slightly to sniff at her, seeing her, but dimly, with its poor eyes.

Petra retreats, screaming. But there are only four places of sanctuary on the floor: her office and the office of the publisher, side by side, with doors that can be closed and locked; and the bathrooms, also side by side. They are closest to her. She turns a corner and slips, badly, in a big scummy pile of droppings, smelling it as she falls. The lamp chimney shatters, the flame on the dwindled plug of paraffin gutters but does not go out. She hears the squealing of frenzied pigs and rolls over in broken glass, gasping, bloodying herself, to see them bearing down on her from out of the dark, so many of the hefty porkers they are fighting each other for room as if, back there where she can't see, pig drovers are hazing them through a slaughterhouse chute. Her screams speak of the torments of hell as pigs surround her, trample over her: she gets up, is knocked down, gets halfway up again—but now some of them are interested in the blood from the cuts on her legs . . .

I'm disappointed in you, Shannon.

Leave me alone.

Very disappointed. I wanted you to draw me, but you drew—

Pigs. Just shut up.

Why did you draw—?

I don't know. They just came into my head, some cuddly little pigs, so that's what I drew. I'm not talking to you anymore. I mean it.

Petra's dead.

What? Oh, you lying motherf—

Are you drawing again? That's good. What are you drawing now, Shannon?

"Something you won't like! Because he'll help me get out of here. And I won't ever have to listen to you again."

I'm afraid . . . I'm beginning to lose patience.

You killed them. You killed them all. Didn't you?

Nobody has ever loved you more than I love you, Shannon.

All those other families, in Nebraska, Missouri—yes, yes, I found out about them!

What else really matters but you, and me, and the music?

"All! All! Dead! DEAD! My family! You bastard! For the love of God, **why**?"

Do we have to talk about them? Sad things make me cry. Your spirit. Your talent. I had to fall in love with you, Shannon. Do you remember when?

"Who   are   *you*?"

We both need to know that, don't we, Shannon.

"You must be Shannon Hill. I'm Robert McLaren."

(The Emerson high-school library. Four o'clock in the afternoon. Shannon is there taking down pictures from the Art Club's annual exhibition. She had thought she was alone, and is startled to hear an unfamiliar voice; but when she turns quickly she recognizes him—at least she has seen him once before that day, in the school offices. He smiled at her in passing. Now she smiles at him. He has a briefcase, an old-fashioned one with straps and buckles. A practice teacher, she thinks, from the School of Education at Emerson State. Several of them are around at the end of each school year, observing classroom procedures. There's a nice breeze coming through the open windows of the library. The dogwoods on the front lawn are the color of clouds, softening the horizon and a blazing prairie sky. Twelve days remain until summer vacation. Soon the Axman cometh.)

"Hello," Shannon says, shaping her greeting subtly, inquiring how he knows of her. McLaren is about six-two, with a well-formed, attractive boniness. He wears casual clothes with a definite flair: navy blazer with buttons like old gold coins and a pocket emblem—two lions in gold thread on their hind legs in mock-battle—gray slacks and loafers. The knot of his burgundy knit tie is a little askew, the shirt collar unbuttoned. He wears his sunglasses on top of a thick head of dark brown hair, razor-cut, which is just becoming the thing for guys, combed a little over the ears. He doesn't look that much older than some of the seniors, but obviously has them beat in self-assurance.

"I was admiring the chalk portrait you did; the one that's hanging outside Dean Elmo's office."

"Ohh—that's my neighbor, Mrs. Mayhew. I'm—well, I'm glad you like it."

"If it's for sale, I want to buy it."

"Buy it?"

"Yes. Don't you ever sell any of your work?"

"Sell any of my work?" *Oh, right, repeat everything he says; you're making a great impression.* "Sure," Shannon says, running a hand through her pixie-cut blonde hair and letting the hand rest lightly on the back of her neck, an almost unconscious gesture that nevertheless makes her breasts a little more prominent. "It's for sale," she decides.

"Then I'd like to talk to you about it. And a couple of other things." He glances at the remaining pictures mounted on portable bulletin boards. "Do you have much more to do here?"

"No, I'll just take those down and put them back in the art room so the kids can pick them up. The custodians'll do the rest, straighten up in here."

"Let me give you a hand."

"Okay. Put them in that pile on the table there. I already have my watercolors."

"Do you ever work in oil?"

"Oh, no. I feel like that's a big step for me. And I like water color. I know I'll give oil or acrylic a try, I'm just not ready. Where do you go to school?"

McLaren smiles. "I graduated from the University of Chicago. Three years ago."

"Oh. You don't look—"

"It's the family gene pool. When my mother was forty, everybody thought she was twenty-five. Never had a wrinkle. I ought to start shaving any day now."

"I guess you're not from around here."

"I live in Kenilworth, Illinois. That's a little north of Chicago, on the lake. Haven't been home for a while, though. I've been on the road since the beginning of April. Six states. No, seven, counting Kansas."

"What do you do, Mr. McLaren?"

"Rob. Let me give you my card."

"Rector and McLaren. Sales Representative."

"Textbooks. You're a junior? Then you're probably using one of our books in American history; that's required your junior year, isn't it?"

"Uh-huh. Are you related—"

"My grandfather was a cofounder of the company. We're one of the oldest textbook publishers in America. I've been learning the business for the last couple of years. Right now I'm in sales and promotions. Before that I worked in the warehouse, and had colds all winter. What I'd rather do is play golf and fly my plane. But I've got a couple of tough customers breathing down my neck: my grandfather and my father."

"How long have you been in Emerson, Rob?"

"Two days. I'll be here the rest of the week. Looks like a nice place. Not that much to do at night, unless you know somebody."

"Bowling. Miniature golf. Movies. Roller skating."

"Where's the best place to go for bacon cheeseburgers? I missed lunch."

"Oh, the Greaser—that's what we call the Greenwood Inn. It's not as disgusting as it sounds."

"Let's go. Unless you're due somewhere?"

"No—I didn't have anything planned. I'd love to."

"Good. But I'm going to make you work for that cheeseburger."

Shannon smiles uncertainly and lightly strokes her hair again, feathering it, wondering what kind of Chicago shenanigans he has in mind. But he unbuckles the flaps of his briefcase ("Used to belong to Clarence Darrow. So the story goes.") and takes out a sheaf of questionaires.

"You could help me by filling out one of these. We collect opinions from the people we hope are deriving some benefit from our books—the students. Keeps us on our toes, and quite a few of our textbooks have been revised according to some of the very intelligent suggestions we get."

"I'm a long way from being Honor Society material—it's a good thing I can draw well, or I know I wouldn't be passing biology this year."

"I graduated *summa cum laude* but I'll tell you something; I never was that smart. I have a photographic memory. Lucky for me; the old man would've disowned my body and my soul if I'd come home with less than straight A's. Tell you something else: a photographic memory has its uses, but I'd much prefer to have your talent. If you keep it up, you could be—do you know who Georgia O'Keeffe is?"

"Do I *know* her! God, she's my hero, she's exactly the artist I want to be some day!"

"We have a lot to talk about," Robert McLaren says gleefully, with the smile that has begun to give her a lovely chill every time she sees it.

They have an hour together at The Greaser, then Shannon has to be home. Time has never gone by so quickly. She knows only a little about him, but when has he had the chance to talk? She's doing all the talking; and Robert, encouraging her, actually seems interested in her boring life. Read any good books lately, Shannon? *"A Farewell to Arms.* I think he's the greatest writer who ever lived. When I got to the end, I just sat and cried for about ten minutes. Then I turned back to page one and started all over. Catherine. You know, it's strange, that's how I see myself. Just like her." Although after a while she is frantic to shut up, mortified by some of the trivial, *juvenile* things she hears herself say (even after a trip to the bathroom she can't seem to calm down), Robert seems reluctant when she must be dropped off on West Homestead Avenue. They sit in his rental car, a sporty Nash Metropolitan, for a few minutes in front of the house, and Shannon is so on edge she

61

has to steel herself not to chew her lower lip, knowing that there is no reason he would ever want to see her again after—

Robert says, "Hey, we didn't talk about Mrs. Mayhew."

"Mrs.—? Oh, you mean—no, listen, Rob, I couldn't sell—I mean, I don't want to sell you the portrait. She lives right behind us, I can do another any time. I'd like for you to have it. It's yours."

"Shannon. That is so beautiful of you."

He leans toward her and gives her a friendly kiss, on the cheek but near the lips, and Shannon, a tingle turning to fire, thinks, *My God, if anybody saw that*—and thinks: *Next time I'm going to be ready.* And without thinking at all she says:

"Where—when can I see you? That is, if you want—"

"Are you going with anybody?"

"No, not steady."

"Do you have a date tomorrow night?"

Tomorrow, tomorrow, what's—Friday!

"No, Friday's perfect. I don't have to be in until—"

"Do you like to fly?"

She has never been in an airplane. "Oh, sure. I love it."

"We'll go flying. It's beautiful over this part of the country at night, when there's a full moon. Sometimes I can even see the shadow of the plane, see it reflected on the surface of a pond when nothing else is moving down there. I think I'd go crazy if I couldn't get off the ground whenever I have a chance. If the weather holds we'll fly out to the Rockies. I love mountains." She is looking blankly at him. "I have my own plane. A Piper Aztec. I've been flying since I was seventeen. I've logged more than eight hundred hours."

"That's great." Now, at long last, she can't think of anything more to say: his accomplishments are humbling, and he admires *her* talent. She has never dreamed anyone like Robert McLaren could exist outside of the pages of *Redbook* magazine. "Well—I'd better go in. It's my night to cook supper." Pork cutlets. Mashed potatoes. When all she wants is to be with him for another hour.

Shannon has barely made a start in the kitchen when the phone rings.

"*Who* was *that*?"

"Oh, hi, Bernice. You mean Robert? Oh, he's a . . . friend, from Chicago. He'll be in town for a little while. You should have come over, I would've introduced you."

"I hate you. I hate you, Shannon."

"It's nothing ser-ious," Shannon says teasingly. "Yet. Got to runnnnn, Bernice."

Robert McLaren arrives at seven the next evening. For one reason or another Shannon's entire family is on or near the front porch. Dab is reading the *Kansas City Star*'s sports pages after supper; Ernestine is smoking one of her rustic-looking hand-mades and carrying on a long-distance, three-way conversation with Mrs. Drewery, who is framed in her kitchen window across the driveway to the left of the Hills', and Mrs. Timrecka on her porch across the street; Chap is mowing the grass; Allen Ray and Duffy Satterstall are throwing a football back and forth in the middle of the street and talking racing cars. A radio is playing the Beach Boys' big hit, "I Get Around." The whole neighborhood is teeming: every kid, every dog and cat seems to be accounted for in the mild blue dusk when Shannon comes downstairs and out to the porch, wincing as her mother shouts to Mrs. Timrecka, "You can't count on me for the auction if I have to get there in Flossie's car!.

The way she drives, I'd feel more secure throwing myself off a cliff!"

Robert pauses to introduce himself to the sweaty Chap, and Allen Ray comes over to see if his sister's date is up to his expectations. "Who's this?" Ernestine says, looking at her daughter as she picks loose tobacco from her lower lip, already a little ulcerous from her long sun-filled hours in the vegetable garden. "Going roller-skating?" But Shannon isn't dressed for a night at the rink and doesn't have her skates with her. She just shrugs. Dab, sitting in one of a pair of chain-hung gliders, the top of his head gleaming like a pumpkin from the bug-repellant lights beside the door, looks at Robert over the top of his newspaper. Dab has a well-chewed matchstick, largely forgotten, in one corner of his mouth. Shannon does a quick side step toward the glider to pluck it away as Robert comes up the sagging steps.

He's wearing sharply pressed chinos tonight, and a Chicago Cubs baseball cap. "Oh, a Cubs fan?" Dab says. He likes the KC A's, but has given up expecting miracles from them. Ernestine says, and Shannon wants instantly to disappear beneath the floorboards of the porch, "Kenilworth? That's kind of a fancy-dancy neighborhood, isn't it? I lived for a time

65

in Blue Island when I was a girl. My stepfather was half owner of a beer parlor there; but for the most part it was just a front for a thriving policy operation." Laughing. "I expect that's all of my shady past you want to hear about."

Her family's flaws and weaknesses are much too apparent to Shannon as she waits for a likely moment to steer Robert to the car and out of the neighborhood: Dab wheezes when he talks and clears his throat often, as if he is going on seventy instead of fifty, Ernestine has left her shoes somewhere else and hasn't given her wiry hair a lick with the comb for the last day or two: it tends to bunch up all on one side. "You'll never know," her mother says to Robert, "how close we came to naming her Ernestine, junior," as if this is a threat she still holds over Shannon's head. She guffaws, in that surprising way of hers— Ernestine, the neighbors say, has a laugh that can unclog a sink. The next few minutes are even more excruciating, but Robert seems genuinely to want to talk to them, to get acquainted, to make himself known as trustworthy and a fit companion for their daughter. He can't help noticing the four-masted schooner tattooed on Dab's left forearm, so they talk about that, and the Navy.

"Just an old sailor man from Kansas,"

Dab says, still amazed by the process that put him in the Pacific for three years. "I was on heavy cruisers—the *Van Damm*, the *Sitka*. Tassafaronga, there was a scrap to remember. Then Saipan, Iwo Jima, lobbing the big shells home. Soon as the weather cleared around Iwo, you could smell those bloody beaches two miles out to sea. Kamikaze finally took us—and me—out of the war. Those were the Nip suicide pilots, you know. They'd load up with munitions and dive straight for your ship. I've got a couple of scars the size of garter snakes criss-crossing my lower back."

"Story time," Ernestine says softly and restively, picking more tobacco lint off her lip. She leans back in a rocking chair to hear Mrs. Drewery a little better.

"I'm saying, Art and me was down at the county tax assessor's day before yesterday, and when the girl asks him his occupation, Art says, loud enough for the whole courthouse to hear, 'Retired sinner!'"

"You wish," Ernestine says jovially.

"We're not like this all the time," Shannon explains, her eyes a little stony.

"What time do you need to be home?"

"Oh—twelve-thirty," Shannon says, not consulting either of her parents.

"No later, I hope," Ernestine says, raising an eyebrow slightly at Robert. "Just going to ride around, see the sights, take in a picture show? Last one at the Empress starts around nine-thirty."

"Late show at the Twin Screens is at ten," Shannon reminds her. She escapes down the walk with her hand in Robert's, ducking as Chap, competing for attention, tosses a mealy handful of grass clippings in her direction.

"I thought it might be best not to tell them we're going to fly over to Colorado to see the mountains," Robert says with a smile.

"You did the right thing," Shannon assures him, her heart beginning to thud agreeably from anticipation. She feels so *daring*. Just flying around the country with somebody she only met two days ago. Bernice and Maryleen are going to flip out when they hear about it—but she'd better get something straight with Rob right away. "Are you sure we have enough time—I mean, seriously, I can't come in at like three in the morning, because Emerson is *dead* after midnight. You know what they'd think."

"Don't worry, I won't disgrace you. It's about eight hundred miles round trip. If we leave by seven-thirty, we'll be back around midnight. Is that for me?" He is looking at the oversize envelope Shannon has under her other arm.

"Uh-huh. The one and only Madge Mayhew. 'Ugly as a tattooed lip.' That's what Dab always says."

The football gets away from Duffy and takes some erratic bounces in their direction; Robert times a bounce, then scoops the ball up one-handed (he has large, strong hands, larger than her father's, which seemed to surprise Dab when they came to grips on the porch). He fires a lofty spiral down the block to Allen Ray, who catches it in full stride over his shoulder.

"I like your family."

"I'm sure they're not a bit like yours," Shannon says with a nervous laugh.

"I hope not." The change in his mood is like a drop in voltage that causes a lamp to grow dim.

In the car as they are driving away Shannon says, "My brother's going to be drafted next month. He doesn't seem to care; but it scares me."

Robert takes a quick look back at Allen Ray. "I didn't do any service. Bad knee. I fell down some stairs when I was eight, and it took three operations before I could walk without a brace."

"Do you know how to get to the airport from here?"

"I know every major street in Emerson by heart, even though I've only been here three days. My photographic memory. I would never need to carry your picture. I'll always remember you perfectly: your eyes are more hazel than blue, although they change to green sometimes."

"All of me is fickle, not just my eyes."

"Your lips sort of squinch up at one corner when you don't believe what I'm saying, like now. And I love the way the lobe of your right ear is bent out just a little—"

"I usually say I slept on it wrong," Shannon replies, touching the faulty lobe self-consciously.

"There's a little fish-shaped scar under your chin—"

"Oh, honestly. Nobody ever notices *that* any more. Now I feel like I'm all scars and bent earlobes. And you won't remember me *always*. I'll bet you won't even remember me this time next year. Maybe you'll be saying to yourself—" Shannon pitches her voice deeper, "—what was the name of that little girl in Whatchamacallit, Kansas?"

"You don't know me. I'll remember. I'll be right back here on this same day one year

70

from now, and take you away in my plane. Only I'm going to have a Learjet by then, one of the first off the line."

"I think we're going too fast already," Shannon murmurs, and with a glance gives him the opportunity to deny it. Robert just shakes his head complacently.

"I keep my promises. I'm very good about that."

The sun has set but the sky is still mildly alight, gold out over the prairie, by the time they reach the airport. Which is no great shakes, consisting of a 3,500-foot paved, lighted runway, a VOR-TACAN cone in a field surrounded by barbed wire, two quonset-type hangers and a small flight service base.

"Okay, you're going to learn a lot about flying tonight," Robert says, eagerly pulling her along to where his red-and-white Piper Aztec is parked and secured by ground cable.

"I have a confession to make. I haven't been up in one of these things in my *life*. And now that I'm this close to it—"

"I've never had any problems. Check that, no big problems." He opens and closes

71

small hatches on the engine cowlings, inspecting whatever is inside. "It's comfortable and pretty quiet too, even with five hundred horsepower. Trust me."

What else can she do, having come this far? And Robert is very thorough—too thorough, after a couple of minutes of technical stuff that leaves her feeling as if she's cramming for finals—explaining how his plane becomes airborne and stays there.

He helps her aboard—one step up to the wing, and inside, where it's as snug as a barrel. Two seats in the cockpit, four more in the cabin behind them. The cabin is filled with stuff: a straw Stetson with a rolled brim and a button that reads *I rode the Blaster at the Iowa State Fair*, stacks of catalogues and textbooks, a long, dusty-looking canvas bag with sturdy leather handles and reinforcement; it sits on the floor between the pairs of opposing seats.

"What's that?"

"Oh, just some of my tools. I'm sort of an amateur stonemason."

Rob shows her his hands, but she already knows how strong they are, and rough, the nails short and scraped and scuffed.

"Friend of mine from college, he took his degree in philosophy but likes working with his hands, a typical son-of-toil Chicago-an. He got me started. I build walls mostly. Do a little sculpting, but I'm not much good at it. My ideas are bigger than my talent. Sometimes I think I'd like to go off somewhere and do another Mount Rushmore. Maybe I will. My mother always told me, 'if something interests you deeply, give it a try.' *Deeply*. Well, that's the way she talked. She was training to be a ballerina, but she grew too tall. She played the violin; wasn't bad, either. A really versatile person. Our house was always filled with musicians. I think she must have given at least a million to the Chicago Symphony. We never missed a concert until just before she died.''

Shannon thinks, *Gave? A million? Dollars?* She says, "Your mom died? Oh, I'm sorry."

"That was a long time ago," Rob says, his smile finishing with a twinge.

Once they are into the preflight runup the thunder of the engines cancels conversation, and Shannon sits back in the snug right-hand seat to deal with her butterflies. There's a certain amount of vibration as their RPM's increase, but Robert's hands move methodically over the throttles and control panel, making small adjustments, Shannon is satisfied that he knows just what he is doing. She closes her eyes when the plane begins to roll. The Aztec takes off so smoothly several seconds pass before she realizes they have left the runway and are westbound toward a vast field of emerging stars, more colorful than she has ever seen them.

"Flaps retracted, gear up," Robert says, then taps the altimeter. "This shows our rate of climb. That gauge tells us how much fuel we're using relative to cruising speed—but we've got plenty to burn. Those pods on the wingtips are extra tanks, another forty-four gallons."

"This is great!" Shannon exults, already over her spate of nerves and not feeling at all queasy. She'd been concerned about what would happen if she had to throw up. In his oversized tool bag, probably.

"Somehow I knew you'd say that," he says, relishing her delight.

Within a few minutes they are at nine thousand feet, leveling off at cruise well below the commercial flightpaths across western Kansas. Rob has a cryptic (to Shannon's ears) conversation with the Wichita Center, filing a flight plan to Colorado.

"Four-niner Echo Charley."

"Echo Charley, good day," the Wichita air-traffic controller says into the headset

Shannon is holding to her ear. Morse code replaces his voice—a VOR station somewhere. Robert taps her on the shoulder.

"Want to take it now?" he asks casually.

"You want *me* to fly?"

"Why not? Slide the seat forward a little. Okay. Those are the rudder pedals under your feet. Left rudder to bank left, right rudder to bank right. *Bank* means turn. Easy does it— she's very responsive. You don't need both hands on the yoke—loosen your grip, you're choking it to death. Good. Let's bank left now, heading zero-three-five. Okay, you're doing fine—bring the yoke back level, keep the nose on the horizon. Shannon, you're a natural. Are those goosebumps on your arms?"

"Yes. You're sure you aren't doing anything—I'm really flying this airplane?"

"You sure are."

"Where are we?"

"You don't have to keep watching the nose, we won't go into a power dive." He studies a map on a clipboard. "Cruising 175 at 65 percent power and we've got a tail wind according to the weather operator, so—we should be thirty miles due west of Emerson and coming up on—well, in another few minutes you'll see the lights of Great Bend off your left wingtip, and Hays to the northwest.

Hang a right at the Pawnee reservation, maintain one-five-zero over the buffalo wallow, and we'll be smack in the middle of nowhere."

"Ha ha," Shannon says. "I love your sense of humor."

"A great night for sight-seeing. See that freight train on the Union Pacific? Four diesels. Must be a mile long."

"This sure does beat roller-skating."

Rob gets out a book of star maps and for half an hour, as they continue west on autopilot toward Colorado, the clusters of town lights beneath them becoming fewer as the sky seems to grow ever-more dense with nebulae, they search for constellations anchored by suns of immense magnitude. With their heads close together, dazed by infinity, by each other's breath, they kiss; and Shannon wonders what it would be like, her first time, up here where she feels far-flung, released from earthbound restraints, from common sense. But Robert's kisses are almost polite and he doesn't touch her suggestively; the momentary notion of recklessness fades with the heat around her breastbone.

Rob makes a course correction. On a whim he reaches behind him for the Stetson and places it on her head. Grinning, Shannon tilts the brim down toward her nose. They hold hands.

"My mother was a nut," Robert says. "I don't mean she was in an institution or anything, she just wasn't *conventional*. She had such enthusiasm, an intensity that just took her out of this world sometimes. And when she was like that, she said she was air-dancing. And I'd ask her what the music was like for air-dancing—Smetana? Berlioz? Tchaikovsky? Those are all my favorites. She'd just smile and say she didn't know, she hadn't heard it yet, but some day she knew she would. Mother either jumped or fell out of the gondola of a hot-air balloon at forty thousand feet; she fell about eight miles. Happened over the Provencal Alps in Southern France. They never located her body."

"That's awful."

"Is it? Awful is dying in bed when you're old and nobody cares anything about you any more. And you've lived your life but you don't know what for. I figured this out once. A body in free-fall travels up to two hundred feet a second. Which means she was air-dancing for almost three and a half, maybe four minutes. I hope she heard it—the music. At least God must have kept her company on the way down, talked to my mother, told her some of the secrets of the universe the rest of us will never find out as long as we're on this earth. That's only fair, don't you think? I believe my mother knew something, instinctively: God doesn't trust us until we trust Him. And we're willing to prove that we trust Him by doing something extraordinary, impossible—impossible for most people, I mean."

"I guess I've never thought of God that way."

"Well, probably I'm—*unconventional*, like my mother was. I just got to thinking about her again, as soon as I met you. Mother would have liked you. I was only twelve years old when she died. Do you know what I did, for the first time, the night I heard she was dead? I shouldn't tell you—you'll be disgusted with me."

"No, I won't. But I think I know."

"After I did it I just lay in bed and cried and cried."

"I think you had a wonderful mother. What's your father like?"

"He's like my grandfather. They're both double-barreled pricks. The best I can say for either of them is, most of the time now they let me alone. I just don't leave any room for criticism. My mother and I used to arm wrestle. Boy, she was tough. She'd never give me an inch. I had to beat her. We sure had fun."

"How long do you think before we get to the mountains?"

Rob switches on the DME to get a distance reading. "Ninety minutes. I hope you're not bored."

"Oh, I'm not!"

"I had a girl once, she was a lot like you. I'm really attracted to your physical type. But she got bored with me, I guess that's what it was, and we broke up. I don't have any real close friends. Nobody who'd wonder about me if they didn't hear from me for a few months. Well, where I grew up you didn't just go out and knock around with a bunch of kids. Parents were afraid of kidnappers. Do you have trouble making friends?"

"No, I still see the same guys I started kindergarten with. We've always known each other and probably always will."

"That's what I like about small towns—maybe I'll settle down in one. But I don't know—I get restless."

Shannon says, thinking she sees tears, "Is it your mother?"

"You can imagine that shook me up. I didn't talk to anybody for a year. I mean, I *wouldn't* talk. All I wanted to do was listen to music. It was all I could do. Symphonies. Oh, a lot of Beethoven. The sound way up. Blasting. I lost about thirty percent of my hearing."

"You must have been—really angry."

"Uh-huh. But I got over it." His eyes are puffy. He takes out a handkerchief. "Sinusitis," he explains, after blowing lustily. "Everybody from Chicago has bad sinuses, it's the weather. Anyway, we have to get over things, don't we? Except for—what happened, I haven't had it so bad. When I turned twenty-one, there was a lot of money. I can do anything I want to do. I'm a lucky guy." Yet he seems confounded, outwitted by a tricky fate that punishes by rewarding. He smiles gamely. "I guess I'm a little hard to understand."

"I don't know that much about you," Shannon says softly, sketching lightly with a forefinger on the back of his hand. Such big hands, but they seem too old to be a part of him: broken nails, an ugly blood blister under one of them. The skin nicked and rough. His hobby: stones, the hammer, the chisel. "I want to know more."

"There's not much left to tell," Rob says, and, as if made speechless by the bitter truth, doesn't try to talk at all for a while.

"I know I want to be an artist," Shannon ventures, thinking it might help to speak of her own deepest concerns. "But lately I've been thinking, maybe that's a selfish attitude. So I'm giving serious thought to the Peace Corps. It's a chance to, you know, broaden my horizons. I've been stuck in the middle of Kansas all my life. But by joining the Peace Corps, it would be like paying tribute to President Kennedy's memory—oh, I know how *stupid* that sounds, but it's what I *feel*."

Her fists are clenched; Robert studies her admiringly, and nods.

"What I can't forget," he says, "Is the look on Jackie's face. His blood on her clothes that she had to wear for hours."

"My mother says she didn't have to wear them if she didn't want to. But that's what my mother *would* say. The assassination just didn't seem to faze her. She has this fatalistic view of things. A church roof falls in on the congregation, a cyclone blows a town apart, oh well. It's almost as if she knows something real bad is going to happen to her, it'll be *her* turn some day. But I couldn't stop crying. Imagine, all that happening on *television*?"

"You know what? The world turned bad the day he was shot. And it's not going to get better for a long, long time. Think about all the stuff that's going on in Mississippi and Alabama. We're going to have another Civil War."

"Oh, God, I know," Shannon says, sniffing. "It's really scary."

"Hey. Want some music?"

"Yeh. We're both getting in some kind of mood, aren't we?"

"Do you know *Dance of the Sylphs*?"

"I've never heard it. Fine. Whatever you like, Rob."

And at last, the Rockies—

In the light of the full moon, most of the peaks still bearing the snows of winter, traces of snows immemorial, the Rocky Mountains command the horizon. At first it appears to Shannon that they can skim across with ease, but as they approach the mountains loom, darkly forested except for isolated gleams of villages, the plane seems to be sinking although the altimeter needle is steady: they are flying at a little over nine thousand feet. She looks up, trying to imagine forty thousand feet. A small and lonely figure falling, with the quickness of a shooting star, toward the white mountain peaks. *God doesn't trust us until we trust Him.* She glances at Rob, who seems different to her, rigid; he is staring straight ahead and the flesh of his face is so pale and close to the bone, could he be searching too, for his mother? And aren't the mountains getting awfully close, blotting out all of the sky? She shivers from a thrill of compassion and, faintly, alarm.

"Rob?"

He is unresponsive. Shannon rubs the back of his hand with her fingertips and that thaws him, frees him from an icy shackle of the mind.

"Are we going to fly over them?" she asks with a timid smile.

Rob's chest lifts, falls. He takes over control of the airplane.

"No. We'd have to go to fifteen thousand feet, almost, and we're not pressurized. You might get a headache, or a nosebleed."

"I used to get those all the time when I was a kid."

"I suppose we could doodlebug the passes through the Sawatch range, but that's tricky at night. I don't like taking chances. I don't like the crosswind we're getting already. Time to go back to Kansas."

On the way home Shannon falls soundly asleep, waking up on touchdown at the Emerson airport.

She smiles at Robert, embarrassed.

"I'm not very good company, am I? What time is it?"

"Four minutes after twelve."

The foyer light is on at the house when they arrive. Hearing them come in, Ernestine calls from the top of the stairs.

"It's us," Shannon says, taking Rob back to the kitchen. "We're just going to get something to eat."

"What did you see?"

"The Rocky Mountains," Shannon answers, smothering giggles.

"Oh. Goodnight. Don't stay up too long."

Shannon feeds Robert the walnut brownies she made earlier. They each have two with big glasses of milk, and when it's time for him to go back to the Holiday Inn she switches off the kitchen light and clings to him in the dark. He pulls gently at the bent lobe of her ear. There's a crumb of brownie at one corner of his mouth that she licks away.

"Tell me you're going to come back and see me," she says fiercely.

"I'll be back before you know it," Robert says. "Remember: I always keep my promises."

You came back, all right! You came back to kill them! Dab. Ernestine. Chap. Allen Ray. And—

You still don't know who I am. But it'll come to you. And then I know you'll want to draw me.

Six. There were six killed in our house! But who else? It should have been me—why wasn't I there?

You were there.

Liar! I would have seen you!

The last time we met, we had so much to talk about. But we never finished our conversation. Why don't you tear up that other picture you've drawn—that fat old man with the beard? Everybody's literary fallen idol. He can't help you. No one else can. Not even Don. Frankly, Shannon—Donald Carnes just doesn't have what it takes. Oh, I know. You almost married him. I know all about your affair with Donald. But I'm not jealous. Now listen. Do you hear the music? The music's important. There's never been any like it. I composed the score myself—for the occasion, when we last met. You heard it then, didn't you? *We* heard it, no one else. Concentrate on the music, then *see*. And draw me. Because I'm getting tired now—tired of waiting for Shannon Hill.

Nooooo! Somebody! Please! Get me out of here, before he killllls meeeeee!

(Silence.)

(More silence.)

(music.   )

Isn't it beautiful? It's all for you, Shannon. Because I worship you.

"Donnnnnnnnnn!"

When Donald Carnes returns from the basement men's room at Cabrera's the rain outside is driving against the windows of the bar, and the lights seem lower, but that just might be an aftereffect of his fourth "Papa *doble*." So, undoubtedly, is the hallucination that confronts him: he actually thinks he sees Hemingway himself sitting on the bar stool next to his.

The rest of the bar is deserted; even Francisco has done a temporary vanishing act. Don is about to make a detour and go out into the rain without his umbrella to find out if a fast walk around the block in the equivalent of a cold shower will sober him up when

Papa turns solidly to him, the seat of the stool creaking under his weight (he's wearing a safari jacket with leather trim, camp shorts and knee-length yellow socks). He grins and swipes at his whiskers with one meaty hand and says, "How long does it take you to shake the dew off your daisy? Get over here, Carnes."

"I beg your pardon?" Don says stiffly.

"You need some help with your problem, and there's no time to waste, according to the signals I'm getting." He seems to have trouble with his l's and r's, a mild speech impediment. "Shannon just hopes you're up to it. Expect that's what I'm doing here."

"You, uh, *you* can't be here. I mean, *he* can't. So what are you, an actor who impersonates—"

Don looks around to see if any of his friends are peeking at him from the dining room or behind the coatroom door. But they are alone, in an unnerving wee-hours silence. Silent, except for the rain and the swish of tires on the street outside. Alone, except for the quick shadowy presence of pedestrians beneath umbrellas hurrying past Cabrera's windows.

Papa slams a fist down on the bar. He is still grinning, testily.

"Watch what names you call a man, unless you're prepared to defend yourself.

Actor? Never had any use for the lot of them, except Coop. And the Kraut, of course. Sit down and drink up. You don't quit after four daiquiris, not when you drink with me. The record's eighteen. At one sitting. You're looking at the record-holder. What we need now are some prawns. You know how I like them: cooked in seawater with a little lime juice, some black peppercorns. But the kitchen's closed." His expression sours. "Makes a man wish he was back home in San Francisco de Paula."

"What problem?" Don says woodenly, edging a little closer to the burly man, anticipating, hoping that he will suddenly laugh or wink or say something to give away the rib, the conspiracy, whatever it is.

Papa just looks at the rain and then at the two of them in the backbar mirror. He lifts his daiquiri and drinks, two good swallows, leaving a little froth on his whiskers.

"Always this spooky?" he says, with a sidelong glance at Don. "Or is it the booze? Not a rummie, are you? I don't mind rummies. It's the bores that make my ass ache. They'd come right in the house, down there in Key West, while I was trying to get work done. 'Just wanted to shake your hand, Mr. Hummingbuffer. Personally I never read anything, but the little lady tells me you're aces. Help myself to your booze? Don't mind if I do.' So what are you staring at, Carnes? Sit down, drink your drink, and we'll roll for the next one. Then you've got work to do."

Don rubs his eyes and his vision blurs; the man in front of him is immediately less substantial. Don, light-headed, is inspired to think he can almost see through him. Panic in his breast. He wants to back away, but is more afraid of the shadowy, empty room behind him than the man on the barstool. Blinking, feeling a chill in his belly that has settled in like a glacier, he eases onto the adjacent stool. Aware he is being stared at, Papa smiles, but grumpily. And Don can smell him: the sportsman's leathery slightly sweaty tang, with a double whiff of sporting dog and gunpowder—did apparitions have an odor? Famous author or not, there is something four-square and trustworthy about him. Loyal to his friends, ruthless to his enemies—why get on his bad side? He only wants someone to drink with, isn't that it? But what is it he's just said about—

Don's fingers curl around the "Papa *doble*" mug in front of him.

"Work?"

"Sure. Your beauty's in a spot of trouble. Not so bad, maybe, if she were alone in that elevator; but she's not alone. He's coming out now, smoothly and cleverly, yet he's in a beastly frame of mind. *Un cabrón maldito*. We will drink now to your valiant beauty, whose valor is not of itself enough to save her, and consider what must be done. Whatever must be done must be done awfully quickly."

Don gulps down a third of the frozen daiquiri while Papa continues to sip his own drink at a thinker's pace, the sun wrinkles bunching at the corners of his eyes.

"Shannon's trapped in the elevator? I knew it! Why didn't Petra call me—I'll call now! The fire department! They—"

"They will be useless to her. By the time they reach her, by prying open the elevator doors, she will be dead. *Muerte*. We are talking now of the Axman, not some ordinary evil but *un malhecho grandioso*—a king of a devil."

"The Axman died!"

"No one can be sure of that."

"And," Don says, confused and sore at heart and scared, "I'm sitting here talking to a dead man too, so I must have got good and drunk when I wasn't counting. I know I haven't lost my mind. There are people who lose their minds and people who will never lose their minds, and I'm one of *them*."

"The Axman may have died," Papa concedes, "but he was never laid to rest. More than a technicality is involved here. None of us are ever truly gone, as long as there is a single memory to keep us alive."

Papa points, as if he is aiming a gun, at the back bar photograph. With no transition Don can be certain of, the flat shadowy cat from the *Finca Vigilia* is crouched cross-eyed and big as life on the bar in front of Papa, who says affectionately, "How are you, you screwy old bastard?" To Don he says, "Meet a forty-year-old cat."

"Aaaaggghhh!"

"If the living recall the dead, the dead will recall the remoter dead, and soon there won't be a decent place in town you can get into. What must be done, then, is simple: keep your beauty from recalling the Axman until she is safely removed from the dark. But no firemen."

Don, looking him straight in the eye so he won't have to look anywhere else, recovers his voice. "Why not?"

"With firemen will come the fire. Which only a king of a devil may survive."

"My God. My God!"

"*Tu lo crea*," Papa says solemnly. "And go now. Before she is desperate enough to draw you."

"Hey, Shannon! Give you a lift?"

(She is walking east on Cottonwood, four blocks from the high school. It is two o'clock in the afternoon on a very warm but pleasant Monday, the first of June. She has one more exam to go—second-year algebra, at eight-thirty Wednesday morning—and her junior year will be over. Then she has three days left to get ready for Dab's surprise party on Friday night. But an even greater surprise is in store: the Axman cometh. He is, in fact, already there. In Emerson, Kansas, in the spring of 1964.)

Shannon has been going over her mental preparations for the party, ticking off expenses. She turns her head incuriously to see who has called to her.

"Oh, hi, Perry—where'd you get the neat pickup?"

It's practically new, a blue-and-silver GMC. But she keeps walking, with only a block to go before she reaches Dab's hardware store, around the corner and three doors down from the main drag in Emerson, the recently named Dwight D. Eisenhower Boulevard. On Dedication Day there was a parade with six bands, fireworks, and an RCA-sanctioned rodeo that night. John Eisenhower was there with his family, but Ike and Mamie sent their regrets.

"My dad's. Actually he never lets me touch it, but he came home drunk Saturday night, fell in a ditch and broke his leg."

"Oh, I'm sorry," Shannon says mildly, but she has no great fund of sympathy for men who drink too much and fall in ditches. As if her attitude is in plain view, Perry Kennold hastens to assure her.

"He hardly ever gets that bad. It was just him and some guys out celebrating, one of them had a kid—I mean, it was his wife who had the kid. So could I take you somewhere?"

"I'm just going to my dad's hardware store to give him a hand this afternoon. It's right there. Thanks anyway."

"How'd you make out in biology?"

Shannon shows him two crossed fingers. "C on the final. That'll give me a C-minus for the year, and I don't have to take *any* more science for the rest of my life, unless I go to college."

"Don't know if I passed or not," Perry confides, leaning out the window, driving with one hand as he rolls slowly along keeping pace with Shannon. "I did okay in English, though. I always do good in English. I just always did like to read. My mother taught me, even before I was old enough to start school.

She wanted to be a schoolteacher once, but then she got married. She had high school and two years of college. She was really well educated. My dad only got as far as eighth grade, and I don't know how good he can read. I never see him read anything, and it takes him five minutes to sign one of his paychecks. My sister dropped out of ninth grade to get married. I don't know why I stay in school. My mother always said she'd skin me alive if I dropped out. But she's not around any more. Aren't you planning to go to college?"

"I'm going to art school in Kansas City—or maybe Chicago," she adds, a recent inspiration.

"If you've got a little time before you start helping your dad, would you like to go to the Dairy Queen? That's where I was headed."

"Oh, I don't think so, Perry, Dab's doing inventory and needs me on the cash register."

"Well, maybe I'll see you again some time this summer. I'm going to work for the Highway Department." He smiles, apparently not caring about the vacancy in his dental arch; he has something to be proud of. "I have to get up at four-thirty in the morning. But I'll be making a dollar-seventy an hour."

"That's good, Perry," Shannon says, opening the door of the hardware store to the accompaniment of a little brass bell announcer. "See you." As the door shuts behind her she leans against it. "Whew!" Maybe he'll get over his crush on her, or just move on when his father's leg heals. But now he knows two places to find her, with school out. Should she give him a big thrill and—no; one of her hard-and-fast rules is not to date boys who drive pickup trucks. The other is more vague but implicit, having to do with status in her peer group and boys with serious complexion problems. She's in love anyway. Last night Robert called, from Pittsburg, Kansas, his last stop on his sales trip before heading home to Chicago. Mentioned something about her coming up for a visit to his family's summer place in northern Wisconsin. Shannon can just imagine what her folks would have to say about that. Hopeless. But in another sixteen months—fifteen-and-a-half months—she will be eighteen, and there are scholarships available from the Chicago Art Institute. In the meantime, she loves being in love.

Dab is angry about something, on the telephone in the office behind the store, or with a customer. Which startles Shannon, who almost never hears him raise his voice.

"I personally don't guarantee the merchandise, because the merchandise comes with a perfectly good guarantee from the manufacturer. I'm saying if you've got a complaint about the quality of that saw, and I must've sold a hundred of 'em in the last six years without hearing another single complaint, then you need to ship it back to the factory. The condition it's in, Leon, looks like it was run over by a road grader or dropped off a roof, and the guarantee specifically excludes that kind of careless wear and tear. You been around tools your whole life, and you know what I'm telling you is true."

"I'm saying this chainsaw's a no-account piece of shit, and I want my money back from the one I give it to in the first place, and that's you!"

Shannon lays her school notebook down beside the cash register and drifts toward the back of the store, which is narrow and deep and only about fifteen feet wide, crammed with floor-to-ceiling bins and shelves, smelling mustily of nails, varnish, raw rope, cold steel. There are no other customers at the moment. She can see Dab with the dissatisfied chainsaw owner, a chronic sorehead and town troublemaker named Leon Burtis, behind the pebbled-glass partition.

"Dab? It's me!" Shannon calls to her father, thinking her presence may cool the dispute, because she's afraid of Leon Burtis and some other Burtises, younger, who are marking time at the high school until they are old enough to be excused from formal education. Both heads turn momentarily, but they can't see out and she can't see in.

Dab says, "With you in a minute, honey." The watercooler belches a big floppy bubble inside the five-gallon bottle and Shannon heads toward it for a drink.

Leon Burtis says, "I don't have no more time to waste on this matter. Do I get my money back or not?"

"Not from me," Dab says firmly.

"Well, you are a cocksucking son of a bitch, and God damned if I'll ever do another dime's worth of business in your fucking store."

"You won't use that kind of language in here as of right now, because that's my daughter outside!"

Shannon steps back from the watercooler near the office door, tilting her head a little to see inside. Leon Burtis has long sun-reddened forearms and his knuckly hands have formed fists. Dab, not small by any means but a couple of inches shorter, just stares him down. Leon's nostrils are flared as big as his ears. His eyes have no definition, they are just an electric blue glow of rage, and sweat beads stand out among the few reddish hairs still sprouting from the crown of his head. Shannon can't swallow; rage and violence in others always chokes her up, freezes her in place. Leon looks at her looking in on him. His taut mouth flinches as if he is going to spit out more choice profanity. Dab won't look away or back off an inch but there is no truce between them, the air they breathe is laced with black powder close to the flash point. Shannon hears the little bell over the front door, but she doesn't look around to see who it is.

Shannon says, "Could I get you a cup of water, Mr. Burtis? You look awfully hot."

Now she has his full attention; before he can say yes or no or refocus on Dab, Shannon quickly pulls a pleated cup from the dispenser and fills it, enters the office as Dab, lowering his hands, takes a step back to make room for her. Once she is more or less in between the two men, the tension of their confrontation lessens and Leon, with a faint show of politeness but no apology, dampens his ire with the cup of Mountain Valley spring water. Then he crushes it in his fist.

Shannon smiles and moves back toward her father, leaving the doorway open.

"We were all sorry to hear about Leona," Shannon says.

He clears his throat and there is something besides rancor simmering in his eyes, not grief but defeat: despite all the anger he can muster, the world will have its way with him. His daughter, a pretty fair barrel-racer, hung around with some of the bigger names in bronc and bull-riding until she was accidentally kicked in the head by a mustang; recently she passed on after two years in a coma. Leon stares at the unworkable chainsaw he has dumped on Dab's desk, is reminded, perhaps, of Leona, clears his throat more loudly and contemptuously, brushes past Shannon and goes quickly down the single aisle of the store, veering past the customer who entered a little while ago.

Dab whistles in a low tone through his teeth.

"Arguing with Leon is like trying to nail Jell-O to the wall."

"I thought he was going to hit you," Shannon says, still worried, a tingling in her hands and around her heart.

Dab cradles his right fist affectionately in his left. "Well, if he had," he says. Dab fought in the navy, and was runnerup in his division, the Fifth Fleet championships in '43. Overweight now, he knows he could still give a good account of himself. But the trouble with fighting a Burtis is that it's like issuing a challenge to the whole clan: they just keep coming around looking for satisfaction.

"Do you want a drink of water?" Shannon asks him.

"I'll get some myself," Dab says, laying a

hand on her shoulder for a moment. "See if you can help that man that came in."

"Sure."

Like half of the adult males in town, their customer on this Monday afternoon is wearing a plain Western-style shirt and jeans, a pair of boots with bulldogger's heels and a rancher's straw Stetson. His hair is coarse and worn in a style known locally as military Mohawk. But, although he has the cheekbones, he's too pale to be tribal. His sleeves are rolled up. He has powerful forearms without a trace of hair on them. His hands are long, but not those of a workingman. They're well cared-for, the nails clean and neatly clipped.

"I wonder if you dropped this?" he says with a smile, extending one of the invitations to Dab's surprise birthday party.

"Oh, it must have fallen out of my notebook; thanks," Shannon says, retrieving the invitation. She lowers her voice. "I wouldn't want Dab to see *this*. Trying to keep it a secret, and so far it's working."

He leans against the counter near the cash register. "Oh, a surprise birthday party." He glances at the back of the store, remembering to keep his voice as low as Shannon's. "Mr. Hill? That's your father?"

"Uh-huh. Dab's going to be fifty."

"That's an important milestone, all right. I'm Autry Smith. Nice to meet you—"

"Shannon." His voice is deep, cultivated. Like a radio announcer's. No placeable accent. Not a Kansan, as far as she can tell, nor a Westerner, although he seems at home in the rig he's wearing. She shakes his hand, looking into his eyes, which are a dark chocolate color. His face is widest at eye level, his brows heavy but plucked, only a millimeter of space between them over his high-bridged nose. He has an easygoing smile and not a tooth out of line. He must be about thirty, Shannon thinks. Unlike the recently departed Leon Burtis, a man furiously at odds with himself and everyone else, Autry Smith has an unmistakable air of competence, even command. So that could be it: he's one of the jet jockeys from the nearby air base, enjoying an afternoon out of uniform. She glances at the class ring on his finger.

"That's not KU, is it?"

"No, West Point."

"Ohhh."

"I'm stationed at Fort Riley," he says, obligingly holding up his hand so that Shannon can get a better look at his ring.

"What brings you down this way?"

"I had some time off, so I'm visiting an

old friend of my father's, Colonel Bark Bonner. He's retired now, has a place ten miles south of here. The colonel's got a bad hip and hasn't been keeping his place up, so I thought I'd do a few repairs." Autry Smith takes a list from his breast pocket, which Shannon scans.

"Just take me a couple of minutes to get all of this together. Would you like some cold water, uh—sir—I don't know what your rank is."

"Captain, but why don't you call me Autry?"

"That's like Gene, right?"

He hums the first few bars of "Back in the Saddle Again," and they both laugh.

"Same spelling, even if I can't carry a tune. Autry's an old family name. We could be distantly related. But I'm from Rhode Island, not Tioga, Texas."

"No kidding," Shannon says, bustling around, picking up flashlight batteries, tape, twine, safety goggles, a hard hat, a hammer, a chisel, and four different kinds of nails, including a quarter-pound of four-inch-long cement nails which she pours into the scoop of an old-fashioned scale on the counter. "You're the first person I've met who's from Rhode Island."

"There aren't all that many of us."

"The ax handles are over there in that barrel. You should pick out a couple you like the feel of."

"Thanks."

"What do you think of Fort Riley?"

"I like it a lot better than where I was last year. Ankara, Turkey."

"You certainly do get around. I guess your family's used to all that traveling."

"I'm not married," Autry Smith says, pulling a hickory ax handle from the barrel and running his fingers along the smoothed grain. "My father was a major general, so I was an army brat. I've seen what the life does to women. I won't get married until I can settle down, earn a living at what I really like to do."

"What would that be?"

"I'm a composer."

"Really? What kind of music?"

"Serious music."

"What instruments do you play?"

"Piano, flute, cello."

"Where'd you find time to learn all that?"

"I never had to work very hard. When I wanted to learn an instrument, I just—picked it up. It's as natural as breathing to me. So is composing."

104

"That's how I learned to draw. Just did it. I've never had lessons."

"Oh, you're an artist."

"Well, I like to think I am."

Autry Smith chooses a second ax handle, glances toward the office in back where Dab can be seen indistinctly, swimmingly, behind the pebbled glass, as if it is one side of an aquarium. He returns to where Shannon is checking off items on his list and puts the handles down on the counter.

"We seem to have a lot in common."

"I'd like to hear some of your music."

"So would I. I've never heard any of it the way it should be played; that would require a full symphony orchestra. The London Philharmonic would be ideal." He shrugs, smiling. "I like the Cleveland Symphony too, since Szell took over. But so far, no one's shown much interest in what I send them."

"It'll happen."

"I know it will. I just have to be patient, and confident of my talent. Get through the dry spells. Well, that does it for me, Shannon, did you find everything on the list?"

"I'm sorry we don't have the three-hundred-pound test fishing line. Not much call for it around here. A five-pound bass down at the reservoir is big news."

"That's okay."

"Let's see—including the ax handles, comes to thirty-six eighteen, with tax."

Autry Smith takes four tens from a money clip with Uncle Sam's eagle embossed on it and hands them to Shannon, picks up the shopping list from the counter, refolds it and places it in one of his shirt pockets. She wonders, fleetingly, why he doesn't just throw away the torn piece of notebook paper; but some people are born savers.

"Do you have a big family, Shannon?"

"Well, there's my mom and Dab, which is short for Dabney, and I have two brothers. Allen Ray's going in the service next month, so it'll just be Chap and me at home then. Chap's twelve. We fight all the time, but he's about the best buddy I've got right now." She rings up the sale and takes the change from the drawer of the cash register. "Here you are. Need a hand getting your stuff outside?"

"No. Nice meeting you, Shannon. I hope your party's a big success. Friday night, huh? Expecting a lot of people?"

"At least a hundred. We're doing a cook-out in the backyard, and I've got a band—it's just some kids from the college, call themselves the Telstars, but they're pretty good. The whole neighborhood'll be there, except maybe the Wurzheimers."

"What's their problem?"

"Oh. I don't know exactly, some sort of feud that goes back to before I was born."

"Well, so long," he says, picking up the brown paper sack, carrying the ax handles in his other hand. Someone else has come into the hardware store, a seventyish woman wearing baggy carpenter's overalls. Autry Smith smiles, crow's feet springing up at the corners of his slightly hooded eyes, tips the rolled brim of his Stetson a little lower over those eyes with the end of an ax handle and goes out the door as the woman in the carpenter's overalls calls to Dab in the back room.

"I hope you're not going to tell me I got to wait another day for my greenhouse sashes, Dabney Hill!"

"They came in this mornin', Myrna. Drive your pathetic old truck 'round to the back and I'll load 'em for you right this minute."

"How's the world treating you, Shannon?" She's a feisty little woman with a bad overbite, which causes her to spray her s's around like Daffy Duck.

"Fine, Mrs. Rockett. That Army man who was just in here, he's from Rhode Island." Shannon always got A's in geography. There is a magic in names and places for her, that prompted her to name the late family hound "Borneo" when she was seven. Some day, renowned as an artist, she will travel to all those places in the *National Geographic* that have caught her fancy.

"Will wonders never cease?" Mrs. Rockett hands Shannon her truck keys. "Darlin', would you mind so awfully doing me the favor? It's double-parked directly out front. I just got to get off my dogs a minute, they're killing me."

"No, problem, Mrs. Rockett."

As she reaches the sidewalk Shannon catches sight of Autry Smith driving by in his station wagon. Now he's wearing sunglasses but he's taken his hat off. In spite of his haircut, he's a very good-looking man. He honks and she waves, thinking wistfully that she wouldn't mind so much being an army wife if you got to do all that traveling. Ankara, Turkey. Wasn't there an article on Turkey in the *Geographic* a few months ago, the splendors of Constantinople? Last night she read about Lapland. With faraway lands spinning through her mind she gets into Mrs. Rockett's truck and puts the key into the ignition. But the truck won't start, it just grinds sluggishly underfoot. Exasperated, Shannon sits back and looks around the familiar street near downtown Emerson, Kansas, and wonders if her time will ever come.

"What's the matter? Can't you get it started? Look, I'm in a hurry, it's an emergency!"

(Eighth Avenue and 33rd Street, New York City. The cold rain is coming down in monsoon quantities now and the battered old cab has stalled in the intersection after the driver was forced to brake for some fool peddling through the rain on his bicycle. The driver wears a white turban that is none too clean, like cast-off bandages, and English is not his native tongue. He shrugs and waves his hands. "Eempossible!" he says, of the junkpile he has been issued to drive.)

"We can't just sit here," Donald Carnes says anxiously, seeing only a smear of lights through the windows, which are thickly awash in the downpour. "Somebody's going to hit us. You ought to get out and push us over to the curb."

"Eempossible!" the driver says, with a cutthroat's glare at the back seat, and Don is thankful for the thickness of the lucite partition, filled with holes like Swiss cheese but more neatly arranged, that separates them. He's not sure where they are, being unable to read a street sign. A bus looms, stops a hair's breadth from the side of the cab where he is sitting, and Don quickly slides to the other side of the bumpy seat, painfully engaging a spring half-sprouted from the stuffing like some evil growing thing. Horns. It's much too warm in the cab, at least the heater has been working, overcompensating for other deficiences all the way down from Columbus and 79th where, fifteen minutes ago, he counted himself lucky finding an empty. The heat, coming after five Papa *dobles* and what he now ascribes to the effects of some sort of drug maliciously slipped into one of the drinks, perhaps by the scary Hemingway impersonator in Cabrera's bar, has him nauseated. Anxiety hasn't done him any good, either. He had not looked forward to a particularly peaceful evening, trying to sort out with Shannon at least a few of the difficulties that had aborted their wedding plans five months ago (*her* difficulties, not his), but now he seems to be in a crisis situation of which he has only a dim understanding, and just about everything is out of his control: Shannon perhaps trapped in an elevator, the possibility of fire (where had that threat come from?), the heavy rain, the stalled taxi—

"Eempossible," The driver says, in a resigned tone of voice. He turns on the ceiling light in the cab and takes a well-thumbed little book from a pocket of his shirt. He begins turning pages imprinted in Arabic or something, as if searching for inspiration or a temporary suspension from earthly cares. Don hears sirens, the deep-throated reptilian blatting of enormous trucks trying to weave through the traffic maze. *Emergency! A woman is about to be murdered in a stuck elevator*! Hairs stand up on the back of his neck. He reaches for his wallet, extracts a ten-dollar bill and puts it in the tray centered in the lucite shield.

"I'm going to walk from here," he says, and is ignored. He turns up his trenchcoat collar, puts on his waterproof bogtrotter's hat and steps out into the slashing rain, confronting a solid two blocks of unmoving traffic, a many-eyed beast of manic displeasure. At the curb and below the level of the clogged street, protected by a yellow tent over a deep square shaft carved through thicknesses of asphalt and rock, the hard hats of workmen can be seen in clouds of saffron steam. Don is momentarily disoriented, not remembering which way is downtown or how to proceed to the Knightsbridge Publishing Company. He splashes through pools of water on the sidewalk to a newsstand, glancing at the face of the proprietor inside his toolshed-size sanctuary, seeing the whites of eyes beneath lids like twisted rubber bands, but no pupils; yet the blind man, anonymous in his muffler and old-world cap, seems to know that Don is passing.

"Time!"

"What?" Don says, hesitating as if addressed, although with so many horns blowing and the fire apparatus edging closer, somehow finding passage through the clutter of other vehicles on Eighth Avenue, it is difficult to hear anything. The old man's face, pale and rugged as a drip-formed stalactite, is turned toward him, and there is a glow in the vacant-looking eyes, perhaps reflections from the little electric heater on an isolated shelf inside the newsstand.

"Getcher time?"

Don removes his glasses to clean the lenses with a handkerchief and wipes rainwater from his eyelashes; he takes a step back toward the box. "Are you speaking to me? I don't under—"

"Time! Time!" the newsie says with a stern upraised finger, and Don lifts his eyes, to a row of magazines under the roof, diagonally secured to a line of wire by wooden clothespins. They are all *Time* magazines, and it is his own face Don sees, or thinks he sees, under the heading "Man of the Year."

Disbelieving, he moves closer, fascinated by the portrait, crudely drawn but recognizable: the chubby cheeks, high forehead, round, horn-rimmed glasses—in the light from a Nedick's window across the sidewalk he can be certain now: it is Shannon's work. But it's only October; doesn't *Time* announce the Man of the Year in their last issue of—

The delayed shock starts somewhere between his shoulder blades and travels with numbing, forked velocity to the brain, exploding in a fireball across the frontal lobes. He tastes the aftermath of electricity in all the fillings of his teeth and staggers, dumb to his surroundings like a newborn, into the path of a couple of black men who, charitably, prevent him from falling on his face.

"Hey, m'man; where you at?"

Don seizes one of them by the wide lapels of his rain-slick leather jacket. "Look. There. See? Who is it? Is it *my* face?"

113

"Hmm. Well. Sure enough is. 'Man of the Year.' Congratulations. Come as a surprise to you, or something? What did you do, make a lasting contribution to world peace? Looks like you been celebratin' too hard."

"Come on, man," the other one grumbles, unimpressed. "If there's been a world peace lately, I ain't heard nothin' about it."

They leave Don leaning against the side of the newsstand, cut across Eighth and the paralyzed body of traffic to Madison Square Garden. Very slowly he edges around to the front of the newsstand and stares into the sightless eyes of the man inside. The blind man's mouth opens in what may be an expression of mirth but which reminds Don unpleasantly of the maw of a rattlesnake being milked of venom. The newsie holds out a copy of the "Man of the Year" issue and Don snatches the magazine, rolls it, thrusts it into a pocket of his trenchcoat. He runs down Eighth Avenue, dodging umbrellas, and as he reaches the corner of 32nd looks back.

Where the newsstand was he sees a growing mushroom of flame and smoke, now two stories high, now three. But the pedestrians on the sidewalk go plodding by in pelting rain as if it is nothing unusual, as if they are totally unaware that something is burning furiously only a few feet away from them.

Don's heart lurches, and then it's his stomach, and he leans over a wire trash basket as everything he's had to eat and drink today comes out in a lurid stream.

There are people who lose their minds, and people who will never lose their minds, he hears himself plead. To a ghost in a bar.

(and I'm one of *them*)

When the retching and cramping of stomach muscles eases he straightens up, using his sodden handkerchief to wipe his lips. He licks at a trickle of rainwater with a vomit-seared tongue, looking around him blankly at the other people in the rain, in doorways, at discarded flowers in a soaked cardboard carton at the curb, flowers waiting for a funeral to come around. The newsstand has vanished, the fire is out, leaving, perhaps, only a small scorched place on the sidewalk. He is not about to go back to see. Slowly he pulls the squashed *Time* from his raincoat pocket; rain has stuck some of the pages together. He crosses the sidewalk to a doorway, already occupied. Old men with stubble who smoke and say nothing. But they make room for him. He slumps down sobbing and

115

peels his way through the magazine to the front cover and is not surprised to see his face is no longer there.

What he sees is a white square with pink splotches as color bleeds through, enclosed by a black border.

Inside the border, these words:

THE AXMAN COMETH

On another fair evening in Emerson, Kansas, creeping up on full dark with the moon, in its late phase, just rising above the trees that line West Homestead, he hears the backbeat of the drummer a good three blocks before he gets there. Already there is no place to park on either side of the street. Judging from the turnout, Dabney Hill's surprise fiftieth birthday party is a smash success.

He changes his grip on the handle of

the heavy square package wrapped in peppermint-striped paper, the package he has been carrying since he left his car half a mile away in a location where it is not likely to attract attention for a couple of days. A car comes down the street, slowly, going in his direction. A dog barks at him from a porch. An old man in his undershirt sits rocking, listening to the radio. A couple of girls are sitting on the front bumper of an old Packard at the curb, gossiping in ecstatic whispers. They glance at him and the birthday present he is carrying and pay no more attention. The rock-and-roll band in the backyard of 298 West Homestead is pounding out a version of "Tutti Fruiti" and he winces. A smoke-colored cat battles moths under a misty street light at the intersection of West Homestead and—he checks the name of the cross street on the white concrete pylon—Columbia Avenue.

He stands there for a few moments, looking down the long block, studying the homes. Fourteen in all. Architecturally it's a mixed neighborhood: one, two, even three-story houses, some set close to the street, some farther back on little terraces. There are turn-of-the-century frame houses with deep front and side porches, gambrels, turrets, paladian windows, a touch of stained glass, television aerials strapped to the chimneys;

California-style brick or stucco bungalows dating from the thirties; big boxy houses of no distinction. Most of these are three stories, with screened front porches and dormer windows all around. There isn't much to separate the houses: a couple of formal hedges along driveways, some post-and-wire fences that probably serve to train climbing roses or trumpet vine. The shade trees are mostly cottonwoods, although a few elm trees remain and look healthy. There's a black walnut or two, and plenty of mulberries: the sidewalks are darkly stained from their maturing fruit.

The smoke-toned cat gives up the moth game and looks at him, eyes picking up some glassy red from the lights of another car behind him. He starts walking again, slowly. The car, an old bottle-green Hudson, stops halfway down the block and a couple of elderly women help each other out: one needs two canes to get around. They have birthday presents with them. They go up a driveway between two houses, one of them saying, "I don't know how much of that I can *take*," no doubt referring to the rock-and-roll band.

He pauses again, looking over the Hill house. One of the big boxy types, but there's no screen on the front porch, just some trellis with pale green vines growing on it on either side of the steps; from the sidewalk, looking up toward the house, which is elevated by perhaps six feet but not on a defined terrace, four front windows on the first floor are visible; but he can't tell much about the rooms inside. The front door, with a tall oval of clear glass in it, is standing half open. From the perspective of the sidewalk or the street no one can be seen unless he or she is standing directly in front of the door. The porch lighting is meager: a couple of yellow bug-repellant bulbs in small fixtures.

He likes all he has seen so far; he likes it very much.

Upstairs, over the porch roof, which is slanted to either side of the house, are five more windows, these with shades, and two dormer windows jutting from the roofline above those of the second story—they are the only windows in the house that are dark. Attic, he presumes, with a generous amount of space judging from the height of the roof. And there appears to be a full solidly constructed cellar, to be expected in this cyclone-conscious part of the country.

By now he can smell food, meat sizzling on an outdoor grill; and the band has temporarily called it quits. He hears the clear ringing of a cook's triangle, a couple of cheers, laughter, someone speaking, unintelligibly to him, into a microphone. There is an amplified, ear-splitting screech, groans, more laughter. He goes up the front walk, separated from the lawn on either side by saw-toothed diagonals of half-buried brick, and up the front steps to the porch. Now he can see through the screen door down the center hall to the back of the house—which, at this moment, with the burgers and hot dogs ready for consumption in the back yard beneath glowing pastel paper moons, appears to be totally empty. He sets down the heavy peppermint-striped package with red-and-white curlicues of ribbon on it and reaches for the screen-door handle. A couple of boys appear at the back of the hallway, jostling each other, making for the stairs at the front of the house, and he steps aside; but if they notice him they pay no attention.

"I'm first!"

"I'm *first!*"

"Why don't you go do it in the yard?"

"Why don't you?"

They battle each other up the stairs for possession of the bathroom. When he can hear but not see them, he opens the screen door and walks inside with his surprise pack-

120

age. There will be people in and out all evening to use the toilet; and probably arrangements have been made with the neighbors as well. It doesn't matter. He needs only a few minutes.

He looks to his left, into a living room that has a trey ceiling, a fireplace with a raised-marble hearth and a Victorian mantel enameled white. There are no windows on the fireplace wall. To his right is the staircase with a center strip of shoddy plum-colored carpet. At the foot of the staircase are sliding walnut doors partly open; inside there is a small lamplit parlor with windows on the front and side, shades half-drawn and covered with lace curtains. He glances up the stairs; apparently both boys have gone into the bathroom and shut the door. He can't hear them. Good thick heavy doors in this house. But he doesn't like the glass in the front door. Maybe there will be a back stairway, the house appears to be large enough.

He goes down the hall, which is darkly wainscotted, also in walnut, and opens a door under the staircase. Closet, filled with winter coats, umbrellas, a couple of snow shovels: the pungency of wool, rubber boots, mothballs. Four more steps to a door directly in front of him, the hall doglegging right to the kitchen. He opens the door. Darkness; a damp, strong whiff of cellar. No need to go down.

He shuts the door, walks into the kitchen. There is a rectangular breakfast table right in the middle of the scuffed linoleum floor. Yellow-and-white checkerboard oilcloth on the table with a lazy Susan. Six ladder-back chairs with cane bottoms around the table. Noisy refrigerator, the enamel badly chipped. Fat water-filled jars on top, each containing a potato that has produced vines in a jungly scatter. He hears the faint downfall of a flushed toilet, hears the boys coming and goes to the sink, runs water, washes his hard, capable hands: he can never get them too clean. The boys pass through the kitchen; he watches their reflections in the semidark glass of the windows over the sink. One of them can't hike his zipper all the way up.

Beyond the porch, which is screened, he can see much of a big backyard filled with people, picnic tables illuminated by Japanese lanterns strung between several trees. The smoky lighting is uneven, with depths to the yard as black as night should be. A temporary dance floor has been laid for the teenagers. There is a long buffet flanked by portable gas grills. The buffet consists of plain fare: platters heaped with buns, bowls of potato salad and relishes, half-gallon jars of mayonnaise and mustard, pitchers of drinks that sparkle in the light. He thinks he recognizes Dabney Hill but can't locate Shannon, even though he lingers in the kitchen for a longer time than is necessary, or wise.

Opposite the sink, a walk-in pantry, crammed with Ball jars that hold big globes of tomatoes, green- and butterbeans, cut squash, rhubarb. Next to the pantry is a door that sticks, but he perseveres and finally gets it open. The back staircase he has hoped for, obviously almost never used, judging from the gray dust on the risers.

He doesn't use this staircase, not wanting to leave footprints. Instead he picks up his heavy package and returns to the front of the house, takes the steps quickly to the second floor. A bathroom, four bedrooms. Four-poster bed in one of the front bedrooms, a sewing-machine alcove, photos on one wall beside a mirror-topped bureau: naval vessels, young sailors in dungarees showing off for the camera, others in battle dress at their stations and all business. A photo of an unidentified aircraft, perhaps Japanese, trailing smoke and inclined at a deep fatal angle toward the brilliant surface of a tropical sea. Another of a group of islands that are little more than barren rockpiles. A reunion photo: jowls, bellies, grins, highball glasses. The centerpiece, large as a magazine cover, is a copy of the famous photograph of the raising of the American flag on Iwo Jima's Mount Suribachi.

Shannon's room is next door, across the hall. Dozens of watercolors brighten the dour mauve wallpaper. She has done several pencil and charcoal studies of Elvis Presley, Ricky Nelson, Fabian. There is a portrait of a likeable-looking boy with batwing ears who might be her brother Chap. Various other teenagers, older relatives or neighbors are represented.

Hoary old stuffed animals tumble against each other at the foot of the bed on the frilly pink chenille spread. The bed is also strewn with articles of clothing, as if she couldn't make up her mind what to put on for Dab's birthday. Her vanity has the usual stuff from Kresge's cosmetics counter. The lipstick is uncapped. So is the nail polish. The styling brush with its gleaning of fine blonde hairs lies on the floor. Her frayed sneakers are under the vanity. So is a Cross-Your-Heart bra. There's a discarded box of tampons in the wicker wastebasket next to the vanity. Shannon is having her period. He digs deeper into the trash, past tissues that have blotted her lips, notepaper on which she has penned drafts of a birthday tribute to her father, and comes up with a used tampon wrapped in a Kleenex. Judging from the heavy flow, she is at the beginning, not the end, of her menses. The horror, the fascination, of women. His excitement is profound. He begins to sense the music. Nothing very definite yet: three notes, then a fourth. D, C-sharp—what else? Never mind, it will grow, the design will emerge.

Someone else has come up the stairs to use the bathroom. The man in Shannon's bedroom has a keen sense of smell, and he detects a cigar. Whoever the newcomer is, he doesn't bother to close the bathroom door all the way while he's peeing. After he's finished he stands in the hall outside the bathroom for a time, clearing his throat, blowing his nose, talking to himself in an undertone before trudging downstairs to rejoin the party.

The man in Shannon's room takes another slow look around, then goes down the hall to the other two bedrooms. Unmade bed, damp towels on the floor of one, a crudely crafted bookcase filled with trophies or mementoes: Little League, Pop Warner football, high-school basketball and football. The remainder of the shelf space is taken up by repair manuals for motorcycles, automobiles and trucks. There is a strong smell of cologne or after-shave in the room. His girl friend in a sugary, blurred-focus studio portrait on his dresser. Short, curly, erythristic hair, long upswept eyelashes, full, parted lips. Allen Ray keeps his condoms (lubricated, reservoir tips) in a cigar box with his cufflinks, tie clasps, a lock of that red hair and a twenty-dollar Saint-Gaudens gold piece. The other bedroom is twice as messy. Stacks of 45-RPM records on a student desk, a half-eaten cupcake in its wrapper sitting on a windowsill, dirty laundry and a catcher's mitt on the seat of the only chair. A bent bicycle wheel and a hula hoop lean against one wall. The only photograph in the room is that of a golden retriever, muzzle thrust affectionately against the cheek of a grimacing, much younger Chap. Copies of *Mad* magazine; horror comic books. Also a paperback edition of *Moby Dick* and a New Standard Revised Version of the Bible, many scraps of paper serving as bookmarks. A report card beside the Bible that shows zero absences and straight A's for the school year. Chapman Hill is, or was, a seventh grader. Under the pillows of his bed is a battered, faded stuffed rabbit in calico overalls wrapped in a T-shirt. Both ears have been reattached clumsily with different-colored thread, a beginner's stitches.

The windows of Chap's room are open, the shades down to within six inches of the sill. He has a limited perspective on the party outside. There is a tentative swelling of voices, then all join in singing "Happy Birthday," the lead guitarist of the rock-and-roll band mercilessly twanging chords. The drummer comes in with a long roll at the end, and a final clashing of cymbals: ". . . tooooo youuuuuuu!" Cheers.

"Speech! Speech!"

There is someone else in the hall outside Chap's bedroom. He cracks the door an inch and looks out. A youth with a ducktail wearing a Harley-Davidson T-shirt gestures to a girl in wheat jeans who stands on the riser just below the top of the stairs. She shakes her head, a little curl falling out of the stiffness of her beehive onto her forehead. He reaches for her, grasps her by the wrist, and pulls her into the bathroom with him. Locks the door.

He has at least a couple of minutes; no one else is on the stairs. The voice of Dabney Hill booms through the house.

"I guess the only time I've been more surprised is when I woke up the morning after my wedding night, and Ernestine says to me—"

But he is interrupted by Ernestine's sink-unclogging laugh, followed by her admonition: "If you tell *that* one, Dab, the next time we all get together will be at your surprise funeral!"

Passing by the closed bathroom door, mindful of some give and squeak in the floorboards there, he hears the boy groaning inside, and the girl says breathlessly, "Let me lick it, Clifton, that'll for sure make it go in easier." Down the hall to the front of the house again. There is a parched rubber plant on a brass stand beneath the window. Next to the master bedroom is the door to the attic. He opens it. Dabney Hill is saying, "—but to be serious for just a minute, if I may, I feel truly blessed to have so many good friends, who have taken the trouble to come by tonight and help old Poop-Deck Pappy celebrate his fiftieth birthday, and I'm looking forward to seeing each and every one of you back here again when the one with the two big zeros rolls around." Applause. He pauses on the stairs; the attic is dark and warm and reeks of stale, settled-in cigar smoke. He takes out his pocket flashlight and searches the risers, looking for obstacles in his way. Then he climbs the stairs to the attic floor, checking the beams for headroom, which is adequate when he removes his rancher's straw.

No windows overlook the backyard, although the wall has been cut to allow for a half-ton air-conditioning unit. Enough light penetrates the grime on the panes of the two small dormer windows on the front of the house so that after a couple of minutes he no longer needs the thin beam of the flashlight to get around without bumping into things: a child's rocking horse and playpen, a mounted deerhead ravaged by moths, a wardrobe filled with out-of-style clothing, twenty boxes of old books, papers, keepsakes, letters, Christmas ribbon and wrapping and ornaments. A gnomelike Santa Claus with a cottony beard and a red-lipped grin. A couple of dolls and doll furniture, a stack of children's board games. An old navy footlocker and seaman's bag, some trunks and other items of luggage.

Dab is saying, "Now I think my daughter has a few words before we get on with the cake-cutting, so all you kids with sweet tooths just settle down, and that goes for you too, Pearl Blaney—"

The attic is unpartitioned. There is the housing of a ceiling fan positioned above the second-floor hallway, a toilet and a sink in

129

the open where Dab has put down some carpeting and made a space for himself, a clubroom of sorts: the centerpiece is an octagonal poker table with the green baize in pretty good shape, a little gray in spots from rubbed-in cigar and cigarette ash. Stacks of chips and decks of cards in the center, glass ashtrays of various shapes and colors all around. Dab has hung a fluorescent fixture low over the table. There is a standing lamp behind an armchair with the fabric worn down to the stuffing in places, a footstool, a little table which holds a humidor and a green glass ashtray the size of a dinner plate, overflowing with ashes and cigar ends. Dab has been forbidden to smoke his cigars downstairs, the man in the attic assumes. Dab has an old pewter spittoon beside the chair. There's half a roll of toilet paper, some Ex-Lax and a sliver of pink soap on the little shelf above the washbasin, which has a big rust-stained blot on the finely cracked porcelain; all of the bowl looks like a blood-shot eye.

For reading matter Dab has stocked mostly hardware catalogues and trade journals, a few copies of sportsmen's magazines, the kind featuring photographs of men with heavy armament posing beside downed grizzly bears the size of King Kong. If Dab is a hunter and fisherman, where does he keep his firearms? That may be a matter of concern. He hasn't seen a gun cabinet anywhere. But he didn't look in the closets in the master bedroom, and he hasn't been to the cellar yet. He will do both before the night is over.

Interspersed between the pages of *Field and Stream* and *Outdoor Life* he finds evidence that Dab's interest in sex is still alive and breathing: a couple of nudist magazines with hale, hearty, bushy people enjoying the sun, and a more explicit, obviously well-thumbed little magazine with captions in Danish or Swedish: a buxom woman pushing her breasts into another woman's face, a man with tattoos, a blacksnake whip and a horse-sized cock lording it over a supine nude; two slightly flabby youths having anal intercourse. Something else Dab isn't permitted downstairs, but who knows the extent of Ernestine's desires, willingness, ability?

Shannon is saying, "For all those nights you were patient with me when I just couldn't memorize the multiplication tables, for all my faults you've overlooked, for all the times I didn't take the time to say, 'I love you, daddy . . .'" Her youthful voice in the gloom of the attic is a thrilling presence, melodious and as suspenseful as a lingering, rising horn call to a supernal, perfect E-sharp; he is inspired, assured that his finest work to date will be done before he leaves 298 West Homestead.

But now he must settle down, find a place for himself. Wait, invisibly, a ghostlike presence in their newly haunted house.

There is some cobwebby space behind the wardrobe, which, he finds, can be moved to make a little more space; and the wardrobe is far enough from the corner which Dab visits so that he will go undiscovered as long as he chooses. He casts around with his small light and finds a straw broom with a broken handle, uses that to sweep out, meticulously, behind the wardrobe, after first tying on a surgical mask to filter the dust. Dust is murder on his sinuses. There are some old drapes in a carton which he spreads on the floor he has cleaned, a couple of cushions left behind when a piece of furniture went to the Goodwill. A makeshift but comfortable arrangement. The attic floor, of course, makes enough noise when he walks around to be heard in the bedrooms; but it's an old house and a windy season, and they have lived in the house for so long they will be deaf to almost any familiar sound it makes at night: floorboards creaking, the branches of a tree rubbing against a gutter or roof. Probably the last thing they would think of is a guest in the attic, in the cellar, in their closets beside their beds with his razorsharp—

Not yet. It is not time to think of this.

"Dab, we love you so much!" Shannon cries out, her voice breaking, and he is touched, almost as deeply as if he himself is the one for whom she has composed this tribute.

Behind the wardrobe he unwraps the package, which contains a toolbag. First he takes out a camp lantern with a nine-volt battery that affords plenty of light in this limited space. The door to the attic scrapes on the sill as it is opened, so anyone coming up will give him warning to shut the light and crouch unmoving in his darkness for as long as necessary. Next he ties on a fresh surgical mask before removing other items purchased recently, before he had a new family in mind. After only a few days in Emerson, and after a few minutes with the irresistible Shannon, his choice seemed inevitable. Ordained. There are five in her house, always the number he seeks. The Cobb family of Briarwood, Missouri, had a pert daughter just Shannon's age. Timmie Cobb. He remembers her now with fondness, for the score they composed together is still his favorite, although, like all the other pieces he's been working on, it is as yet unperformed. There is time for that, he reminds himself. He is a young man, still growing in his art. What matters now is the vital, the daring act of composition, doing the groundwork, tapping deeply the streams of inspiration that families like the Cobbs, the Crismons, the Hanyards have provided.

Out of his toolbag comes a mechanic's one-piece coverall, a hard hat, polycarbonate safety goggles, driving gloves to protect his hands from blisters. A four-pound hammer with one blunt and one tapered, cold-forged chisel end. Nippers. A new hickory ax handle to replace the one that was broken during his last home visit. He is never without at least one spare ax handle. His kit also contains two double-bitted ax heads, the curved, sharp edges protected by tough leather scabbards. And duct tape, cement nails, used but not worn clothesline, the fishing line he has found to be more reliable than ordinary baling wire. The husky Hanyard boy, cheating on the finale, somehow broke the wire that bound his wrists and, weakened as he was by loss of blood and handicapped by having no feet, still almost managed to crawl out of the house alive. As it was his work was botched, the ballet score had to be discarded. His disappointment left him in desperate shape for a while. This happened in Iowa. Crestview, Iowa, where neighbor trusted neighbor and no one bothered to lock their doors or windows. He has assumed, on his drives through town, that Emerson is that sort of place, too. He's found it very friendly so far. He feels very much at home here.

Now he takes time out to review all of his movements of the last twenty minutes, when he arrived on West Homestead Avenue. He hates mistakes. The discarded surgical mask? Right there in the pocket of the tool bag. He has total recall of every step he's ever taken in each of the four houses he's visited to date. A fat memory book to browse through. But it hasn't been all fun. There are always surprises to deal with. And he can't face the prospect of another botched, useless score.

Might as well change clothes now, while the party is still going on. He isn't so sure it will be tonight, but there is no sense in not being prepared. So off with the Levi's and boots and the shirt with the mother-of-pearl buttons, adequate camouflage wherever he wanders in the Heartland. He folds and places this clothing neatly in the box. He is wearing white Jockey underwear briefs and white boot socks that come to just below his knees. On the right knee, the trick one, is a protective brace. He pulls on the roomy mechanic's coveralls and does up the snaps, then laces on a pair of bowling shoes; they are light in weight and afford a maximum grip on tile and hardwood floors—some women just can't get enough of waxing their floors, and fresh blood on a newly polished floor can be greased lightning. But from what he has seen of Shannon's house, Ernestine is at best a desultory housekeeper.

When he is dressed he prepares his ax, using the four-pound hammer to pound a bit tightly down onto the handle. Hearing the rock-and-roll band again, he wishes he'd brought along earplugs. It's the kind of music that puts him in a baleful mood—ugly, edgy, prone to mistakes, to doubts about the sanctity of his pursuit.

Do you remember that night, Shannon? How well do you remember?

*Can't remember. They're all
dead and I don't want to remember*

Oh, but you must. It's inevitable. So is
the work we'll finish, together. Before the
night ends.

"Help me help somebody!!! I
can't take any more "

I don't want to die!

You know that I can get you out of the
elevator. I'm the only one who can. Be sensible.

"Stop torturing me "

Is it torture to be loved? Adored?
Needed? I need you desperately, Shannon.

"No   way.   You're   not   coming back."

The   way   out   of   here,   Shannon,   is through   the   back   door   of   your   house   in Emerson. You're so close now. The party's over. Just walk inside. And I'll be there.

"I can't go in the house!"

Of course you can. It's home, Shannon. Come on."

"Come on, honey."

"You okay, Dab?"

"Sure. But it's been a lot of excitement, and   I'm   feeling   kind   of   tired.   I   think Ernestine's hit the hay already."

"What about Uncle Gilmore?"

"He's happy," Dab says. "Let him be."

They pause in the back yard, arms around each other, and look at the lawn glider with the fringed vinyl top. Gilmore Hill is sprawled on the glider, his appaloosa-hide Stetson cocked low over his face, a cigar in one hand, a paper cup in the other. Uncle Gilmore brought his own refreshments to the party, and the fifth of Jack Daniels black label is about empty. For the last half-hour he's been singing softly to himself all of the hoary Western songs he knows.

"Need anything, Uncle Gilmore?" Shannon calls to him.

"Doin' just fine," the old cowpuncher replies, waving his cigar in the air. "Believe I'll catch a couple hours' shuteye on your sofa in the living room, light out about four a.m."

"Might as well stay for breakfast," Dab says. "No telling how long before we see you again."

"No, no, thanky; fix my own breakfast, that is if Ernestine don't mind my puttering around in her kitchen."

"You're more than welcome, Gilmore."

"I'm gonna be sixty next time around. If you think fifty's a bad idea, wait 'til you hit sixty."

"If you run shy of potables," Dab says, "look in the sideboard in the dining room. And thanks for coming."

"Why don't you sit down here, and we'll have a talk."

"Long past my bedtime, and the doc says I've got to get my sleep if I'm going to lick this blood pressure."

"I always won all the marbles when we were kids; and you never have got over it, have you, Dabber?"

"Hell," Dab says, good-naturedly, "keep the marbles, Gilmore. Just pay me the World Series bet you owe me."

"Which World Series?"

"'59. The Dodgers in six, just like I predicted."

"You know good and goddam well I paid you that fifty dollars."

"Suppose we separate the flyshit from the pepper here and now."

"Dab," Shannon says gently, squeezing him at the waist, "blood pressure."

"I always said they ruined the game forever when they let the niggers play."

"Oh, hell," Dab says under his breath, "he's just on a toot and there's no sense trying to talk to him. I'm going up." He busses Shannon's cheek. "Thanks for everything, honey."

Shannon scratches a mosquito bite on a bare ankle, then picks up a piece of ice Allen Ray has dumped out of a washtub as he and

Duffy clean up the backyard. She applies the ice to the lump.

"I'm just glad you had a good time. Mom always says, show you a roomful of people and you get the gruffies."

"Well, I've got this loner streak in me. Not all that sociable. Runs in my family, as you can see."

"Where do you want me to put all the presents?"

"Handkerchiefs and neckties, bedroom I guess. You can do me a favor and carry those boxes of cigars up to my hidey-hole tomorrow."

" 'Bury me nottttt on the lone prayer-eeeee—' Have a nightcap with me, Dab?"

"You know I don't drink hard liquor."

"You never have got over the fact I could whip your heinie any time I felt like it."

"I'm just appalled by your ignorance, Gilmore."

"I don't know why I drove all the way down here. I must have ticks in my brain."

"Nice seein' you again, Gilmore. Give my best to Zelma and the perennially unwed Auline."

This he says in a lower tone of voice; Gilmore doesn't hear him but Shannon has to turn away with both hands over her mouth to keep from belly-laughing. Dab winks at her and trudges off toward the porch. Allen Ray and Chap saunter over. Allen Ray says, "We'll take those lanterns down in the morning."

"Thanks, Allen Ray."

"It's early yet. Think I'll pick Sondra up at Patty Ann's and we'll knock around."

"Just don't knock her up," Chap says, and takes off at top speed with Allen Ray and then Duffy in pursuit of him. "Don't you ever get tired of doing it in *cars*?" Chap says gleefully over his shoulder as he disappears around a corner of the garage and hops the fence into the Drewerys' yard. "She's got freckles on her *butttt* she's pretty!"

"Uncle Gilmore, going to stay outside for a while?"

"Might as well, Shannon. Seeing as how nobody appreciates my company."

"Well—I'll put a blanket and pillow on the couch for you, and if I don't see you in the morning, have a safe trip home."

Inside the house Shannon takes a critical look around the kitchen, which isn't too bad: a couple of their departed guests have pitched in to fill several garbage bags and stack rinsed dishes beside the sink. She'll finish the job in the morning. Outside, Chap yells; Allen Ray has flushed him from hiding and she wonders if she ought to interfere. But, no, if Chap is big enough to smart off at the

142

mouth like that, then he's big enough to accept the consequences. Shannon's feet hurt. She loves going barefoot, although this usually results in cracked heels before the summer is over. Twice tonight her toes got walked on. She sits down gratefully with a bottle of NeHi orange, rubs her ankles and calves.

Allen Ray takes off out of the driveway, exhausts burping noisily, tires screeching, getting the most fun out of his four-barrel and Hurst speed shifter. Shannon yawns and smiles to herself, thinking how nice the party was. Entirely up to her expectations, and Dab had a glow around his head that must have been visible from the planet Mars. Now she can't settle down. She doesn't want to watch TV. A cramp is coming on, a big one; and she's still flowing heavily. She goes upstairs with the bottle of soda and looks for Midol in her room. After she washes down a tablet she goes down the hall to the bathroom with her pajamas. Strips and takes a warm sponge bath in the tub, douches, then inserts a fresh tampon. She thinks about women of bygone days and how they had to cope. A real curse then. Yards and yards of muslin. Old photos of frontier families in front of sod houses, the women are never smiling. No wonder. Spot on her underpants, she rinses it out and hangs the panties up to dry. Puts on a clean pair, then her pajamas. Breasts tender but the cramps fading. When she comes out of the bathroom she sees Chap lying down in his room reading a comic book. Dab is stealing down the hall toward her, a couple of Cuban cigars in his fist, a guilty grin on his face.

"Just one before I turn in."

Shannon takes a blanket and pillow from the hall linen closet and goes downstairs to the living room. Uncle Gilmore is still singing to himself in the backyard. She decides to leave the porch light burning so he won't fall and break his neck getting into the house. She also leaves a lamp on in the living room and goes back upstairs feeling a little tired now, but not sleepy. Maybe she ought to wash her hair; but if she does, in the morning it'll look like a fox got into it. She straightens up the room, decides to write a letter to Robert McLaren, although she has high hopes of seeing him again very soon.

Above her head the attic floor creaks, creaks again. Dab. Halfway through the letter she's composing she can't keep her eyes open.

Shannon puts the pink clipboard aside and turns out the reading lamp clamped to the wrought-iron headboard, pulls the sheet over her, stretches out catty-corner and facing the windows. They are raised a few inches and a cool breeze comes in. Uncle Gilmore's raspy singing voice has faded to a drunken mumble. The attic floor is still creaking. Cottonwood branches gently scrape the gutter above her windows. The breeze, stirring leaf against leaf along the street, makes a sound like a soft and distant rain falling.

She is asleep when at last Gilmore comes stumbling up the porch steps into the house, asleep when Dab comes down from the attic drenched in the smoke from a choice cigar and enters the bedroom opposite hers, asleep when Allen Ray arrives at a quarter past one and takes a shower.

But at twenty-past-two, when everyone else is sleeping, Shannon is awake.

The breeze has strengthened to a wind, shadows criss-cross the flopping shades, she feels cold in her cotton pajamas. She is lying on her side with her knees drawn up, hugging a pillow. Other than the wind and the crinkle of the in-blown shades, the only sound she identifies is the tick of the clock on her dresser. But there is a prickling of fine hair on the back of her neck; instinctively she knows she is not alone and sits up suddenly, holding the pillow defensively against her breasts.

"Hey," he says softly.

"What? 'sthat?" Then she smells him, a little of dried boy-sweat, and spice from old cinnamon chewing gum. "Chap?"

The mattress sags as he crawls onto the vacant side of her bed.

"Can I sleep with you?"

"Why?"

"I just feel like some company."

"Okay. You can't get under the covers."

"How come?"

"Because you kick like a G.D. mule. Last time I had a bruise on my thigh for a week. Not to mention you never trim your toenails."

"Oh." Chap crawls to the foot of the bed and begins rummaging through the animals there.

"What are you doing?"

"Looking for something to sleep with."

"You're too big to sleep with stuffed animals."

"How come you still have all these?"

"Sentimental reasons. Besides, I'm a girl. If you want a stuffed animal, why don't you go get Bubber-Bunny?"

"I don't have Bubber-Bunny any more. Mom threw him out."

"I'll bet she did. Bet you got him back, too, since you're always going through the garbage."

"I have to protect myself."

"So go get Bubber-Bunny."

"No, I don't want to go back to my room. Can I have your elephant?"

"You may not. Elefunk is—personal. Elefunk is for when I'm feeling lousy and need to have a good cry."

"I'll take this one."

"Which one?"

"Feels like a bear."

"Okay. Settle down, will you?"

"Could you close the windows?"

"*Yes*. Any more requests?"

"Huh-uh."

Shannon gets up to close the windows. From below there is an intermittent disturbance like a buzz saw working its way through a mountain of clotted cream. "What in the world is that *noise*?"

"Uncle Gilmore snores. Woke me up."

Above them the attic floor creaks.

"Been doing that," Chap says.

"Dab's probably—"

"He went to bed a long time ago."

"Since when does the floor need a reason to creak? This house is forty years old. If you wouldn't read those old horror books before you go to bed, you wouldn't get scared."

"Who says I'm scared?"

Shannon gets back into bed, shivering a little, pulls up the spread, turns over. "Want some covers?"

"No, I'm hot."

She gropes and finds his face, palms his forehead. "You're running a temperature."

"Hey, don't."

"Why, does your head hurt?"

"Allen Ray gave me a knuckle rub. *Yes*, it hurts." Suddenly he is crying.

"Aw."

"Sometimes I hate—Allen Ray."

"No, you don't."

"He's so stuck-up I can't talk to him any more. We never—do anything together. He's out every night."

"Well—Sondra takes up a lot of his time. So does racing. I wonder if you're coming down with something. You don't sound stuffy."

"I just get hot at night sometimes."

"I used to. It's puberty, I guess."

"It's what?"

"Remember when you had growing pains? This is—a different sort of growing pain. You're not going to be a kid much longer."

"Oh. I know what you mean. I don't have any hair yet, though. Down there."

"Another year. Why don't we try to go to sleep?"

"Shannon?"

"Huh."

"Hold my hand."

"You're hard to please tonight. You need a bear, you need to hold my hand. Here."

"I just don't feel good."

"How many hot dogs?"

"Four. I think."

"With pickilily? Big gobs of pickilily, I bet."

"Yeh."

"No wonder."

"I love you. Good night."

"Good night, Chapman. And good night to *you*, Uncle Gilmore; please put a cork in it."

Four-oh-five a.m.

Gilmore Hill sits up suddenly on the living room couch, having snorted and slobbered himself into a state of conditional wakefulness. Earlier he had a lot to drink, but he is accustomed to heavy drinking, then rising from long habit well before dawn.

He knows instantly that he is not alone downstairs. Clears his throat and mutters, "Who's there?" His eyelids are sticky and he rubs them, turning his head just in time to catch a fleeting glimpse of someone in the hall. It is still full dark outside, no cockcrow as yet, no restless dogs or lovelorn cats disturbing the peace of West Homestead Avenue. The moon is in its last phase, but enough street-shine comes through the oval of glass in the front door and the partly shaded living room windows to give definition to doorways, picture frames, furniture, the curve of the bannister at the foot of the staircase.

He saw someone, all right, disappearing in the direction of the kitchen. Not Ernestine. And too slender to be Dab. One of the boys, maybe the younger one—Chap?—with the morning paper route. Gilmore is unaware that the local paper, which Chap delivers in partnership with Aaron Wurzheimer, does not have a Saturday edition. He cannot know that Chap is fast asleep, bundled up against his sister in Shannon's bedroom.

Gilmore reaches for an already well-used paisley handkerchief and attempts to clear his sinuses, a futile task after nearly a fifth of whiskey. His throat feels and tastes like rust. Without putting on the boots he has left beside the sofa, he gets up, his knees popping painfully, and gives his stiff left shoulder a probing massage before proceeding to the dining room and then to the kitchen to put coffee on, such an ingrained routine he hardly notices, at this stage of wakefulness, that he is in another man's house. Until he discovers the six-quart enameled pot is not on the back of the stove where it usually is. Shit. Looking around but he can't see much, and doesn't know where to find the light switch. Holding himself now below the belt because all that whiskey is like an ocean in his bladder. The nearest relief is off the back-porch steps. His prostate enlarged by years on horseback, it takes a while to void. Dribble, dribble. Shakes it in a melancholy way, stuffs it back behind the fly which he doesn't bother to zip up and returns to the kitchen. Where do they keep the damn coffeepot around here? Two doors. One sticks. He quits tugging at it, turns to the second door, opens it. Pantry. Oh, and somebody's in there.

The shock nearly blows the gaskets out of Gilmore. His mouth flies open but he can't make a sound. He stares for a second too long at a hard hat, at clear plastic goggles. At the man, moving, hands coming up chest-high; and at the butt end of an ax handle. Of the ax itself he has only the merest glimpse and no chance to react as he is struck in the throat above the collarbone notch. His larynx is crushed. The blow sends him straight back as if whiplashed and crashing down on the kitchen table seven feet away. Pain ignites his brain as he struggles, futilely, to breathe, rolls slowly to his right off the table and fetches up on all fours on the floor. Collapses as he raises a hand to his broken throat. Sees, standing over him, the axman, goggles a glassy gleam, shoulders lifted for the forceful stroke. The ax, when it appears, is not even a blur, just a sharp curved sliver of light that is mysteriously, secretively *there*, then gone, in a fraction of a second before his scrawny body is jolted as powerfully as if he has been hit by a car. The back of his head strikes the floor, his feet fly up, and before his heels touch the floor again, Gilmore is dead.

The bedroom directly above the kitchen is Allen Ray's. He is ordinarily a sound sleeper, and has been known to go on snoozing peacefully after being pulled, bedcovers and all, to the floor. Tonight he had sex (twice) with Sondra, which relaxed him greatly. But the clatter and thumping in the kitchen is sufficient to cause a vibration, as if the house has been jolted by an earthquake. The sleepers in the front of the house are not aware of the momentary disturbance, but Allen Ray, roused from a dream of foggy dirt tracks, bugs as big as flying mice around the light poles and battered cars in a slewing, fender-to-fender finish, sits up befuddled, wondering what he heard or if he heard it. The luminous hands of the big alarm clock on his dresser tell him that there is still more than an hour to go before dawn.

Allen Ray sinks back in a daze, limbs heavy, and he would be almost instantly asleep again except for a couple of physical distractions. His mouth is still very dry from French-kissing, his tongue sore where Sondra, in her excitement, bit it. He is momentarily suspended between the urge to plunge back into sleep and a craving for a cold quart of milk. Once he begins to actively think about the milk the prospect of sleep recedes. Allen Ray sits up again, stretching. Four-thirteen a.m. He is naked except for the pair of clean boxer shorts he pulled on after taking his shower. He stands up, takes a couple of steps toward the door, stumbles over the wet towel he dropped on the floor earlier, kicks it aside and goes out to the hall.

The shortest distance to the kitchen is by the back stairs, which, for some reason, the family members seldom trouble to use. For one thing, no matter how many times Allen

Ray and Dab have worked on it, the door on the first floor doesn't open easily. It is necessary to apply upper pressure on the knob with one hand, then push with the other about three-quarters of the way down on the right side. Easier just to go the long way around, particularly if you're carrying a load. But Allen Ray is intent on getting back to bed quickly. He takes the backstairs and goes through the routine of springing the stubborn door open, which on this occasion works like a charm. He is two steps into the kitchen on his way to the refrigerator when he becomes aware that the pantry door is standing open, a chair is overturned, there is a sharp odor of vinegar in the air from a broken cruet on the kitchen table. And someone is lying on the floor on the other side of the table.

Allen Ray, sharp-eyed, heart leaping high in his throat, identifies him immediately: Uncle Gilmore, who was slugging down the Jack Daniels all evening. Now he's lying there passed out, or worse. Because he's so *still*. Allen Ray can't swallow the lump of his heart —his chest has constricted, there's no room for it. His face feels cold, the back of his neck tingles.

Better get Dab. But if Uncle Gilmore is only sleeping, not unconscious, then—

154

He circles the table, staring at the up-turned face. Oh-oh.

Gilmore's eyes are open. His mouth is open too, the lips dark, and there's a dark stain down his shirt front, as if he's spilled whiskey or vomited all over himself. But Allen Ray should be able to smell it if it's whiskey-puke; no, what it looks like—

Allen Ray turns, lunging at the refrigerator. Knocks a lot of the little magnets off along with Ernestine's penciled reminders to herself and other family members as he snatches open the door and looks back at Uncle Gilmore.

God dog it *is* blood! Gilmore's drenched in it. Blood is welling from some sort of large hole or gash right down the middle of his chest. Perhaps as recently as a minute ago the split heart was spurting, because in the light from the refrigerator there are stipplings everywhere: on kitchen cabinets, the linoleum floor . . . the ceiling drips.

Allen Ray is only nineteen, but he has courage; it is something he has always taken for granted. The ability to act coolly in a crisis. He has proved himself in football, in fistfights, in racing. Unfortunately there is no precedent for the horror he now faces: a newly dead man, probably murdered (although this dangerous factor has not yet registered in his stunned mind), in the most familiar of surroundings. He is enveloped in a billowing mist from the refrigerator, yet colder than anything on ice. Sickened, too. He knows he must do something, get help. His most powerful impulse is childlike, inevitable—to run away. He stiffens and resists the impulse, fights it while the time for decision-making ticks away and the Axman cometh.

Four-fifteen a.m.

In her bed at the front of the house, Shannon wakes up as Chap, made uneasy in his dreams, convulsively tightens an arm around her. True to his style, he has pushed her nearly to the edge of the bed by the windows. The sheets are in a tangle. She pushes him back to somewhere around the middle of the bed. On his back, the mildly asthmatic Chap begins to snore.

Shannon fussily straightens out the covers, then presses a pillow around her head so she won't hear him. Glass shatters in the back door of the kitchen, but she doesn't hear that, either. Nor the liquid coughing sounds that Allen Ray, with his throat sliced open, makes as he tries to pull his arm free of the glass shards and attempt a last desperate run for his life.

Four-eighteen a.m.

Chap snores, one foot thrashing.

Shannon dreams.

In the other bedroom at the front of the house, Dab with his cigar breath burbles, not unpleasantly, in his slumbers on his side of the bed. Ernestine, on her stomach, a hand trailing nearly to the floor, is soundly in the grip of her favorite tranquillizer, a heavy shot of vodka—two shots tonight, one shortly after retiring to their room, another an hour later when she realized, what with the ache in her prematurely old knees, that she wasn't going to be able to sleep without another friendly infusion.

Dab has known about the vodka, which Ernestine keeps in a hatbox on the back of the closet shelf, for a long time. Worries about it, but doesn't say anything.

Four-nineteen a.m.

A creaking on the back stairs that no one hears.

The Axman Cometh.

"Carnes!"

It's him again. Papa. Old Humming-buffer. Don tries to ignore his presence—wherever he may be. The rain won't quit and the city, at least this part of the city south of Twenty-Fourth Street, is in blackout. There is traffic on Sixth Avenue, proceeding very slow-ly through intersections, headlights of taxis and buses. But there are only occasional vehicles on the cross streets, Eighteenth and Nineteenth, that bracket what had been, in more gracious times for the neighborhood, the Woodrow & Lavont department store. Elegance is apparent in every line of the architecturally significant building, despite recent abuses. Since he arrived, walking and sometimes running all the way down from Thirty-Second Street, Don has worked his way around three sides of the building looking for a way in. All of the metal doors he has located require one or more keys for entry. Accessible windows are blocked by wire grills bolted to stone. The former store's large, street-level display windows deep within the facade and facing Sixth are boarded up, plastered over with several years' worth of handbills. Where double revolving doors once admitted women with parasols and men in derbies and spats, the entrance is now through a plywood tunnel blocked by an iron gate. No watchman is on duty; at least he hasn't been able to raise anyone by repeatedly rattling the gate, banging on side doors. Calling until he is afraid his throat is about to give out.

The temperature is still dropping; Don's thoroughly soaked and shivering, and he's always been susceptible to bad colds at any sudden change in the weather. Already he's woozy, beginning to feel feverish. At least it's dry under the facade, which is supported by thirty-foot bronze columns on granite bases as high as his head. But what is he supposed to do now?

"Don't overlook the obvious," Papa says, closer but still somewhere behind him.

Don sneezes into a damp handkerchief, sniffs forlornly, looks around as the headlights of a passing bus illuminate one of the fluted pillars, the size of a young redwood tree, and the wise old hunter standing at the base, buttoned up to his whiskers in foul weather gear, cozy and at home in the elements.

"What do you mean?"

"Fornicating rain's coming down hard. Plenty of homeless in this burg. Where do they all go to get in out of the rain, get warm, grab a night's sleep?"

"Subway."

"Use your canoodle. What did Miss Petra say about this building when you talked to her?"

"She said—oh, I get you. She said there were some unfinished floors, and she thought probably some derelicts, or maybe drug addicts, are holed up on those floors. But I haven't seen—"

"Haven't seen any rummies under this facade, even though it's decent shelter. None of their usual trash, either. Rummies leave their bottles where they empty them. They piss where they've a mind to. Piss on stone, it soaks in, stink rises whenever it rains. Ought to smell like a cageful of cotsies under here, but there's no rummy spoor. What does that tell you?"

"I . . . I don't know."

"I walked away from a plane crash with spinal fluid leaking out of my ears, and I could still do a better job with what brains I had left than you're doing tonight."

"Thangs a lod," Don says resentfully, and blows his nose again. Too hard. His ears block. He looks helplessly at the plywood runway, the padlocked gates, and thinks of rummies.

"If there're any inside, then . . . they must have a way in I didn't think of."

"While you were busy trying to kick down locked steel doors."

"Maybe—an alley—"

"The only alley in Manhattan is Shubert Alley. They didn't tunnel up from below the street, either."

"I'll . . . have another look around."

Papa lays a finger against his nose. "Follow this," he suggests.

"What?"

"Rummy spoor."

161

"I can't smell a thing."

"Maybe I'd better go with you this time. Tracked a lioness in heat through the rain in the Serengeti. Her spoor was like attar of roses, compared to a rummy's."

"Don't you talk to bears, too?"

"When I happen to run into one. We'd better move quickly now. Your beauty is weakening, and he's stronger. He'll know I'm around. He'll know how to get rid of me, too."

"I don't know why I believe any of this."

"Because you believe in the Axman. She's made a believer of you, all the years you've known her."

"If only I'd married Shannon. I should never have let her get away with jilting—"

"She was trying to protect you."

"But he must have died! They found his blood in the house. And after Kansas, there was never a sign of him."

"He's been living in the one place that's safe for him," Papa says.

They are on Eighteenth Street, walking east, toward the rear of the large building. A cab, off duty, hisses toward them, throwing up a wave Don can't avoid. Turning, he sees no one, although Papa has been right behind him. After the cab passes he looks up and is startled to find the author twenty feet down

162

the sidewalk revealed in the counterglow in gleaming rainwear, moon-shaped face pressed close to a wall thickly papered with dilapidated one-sheets promoting opera, ballet, a reunion at Town Hall of folk artists from the sixties.

"Nope," he says, stepping away from the wall as Don jogs soddenly up to him, his expensive shoes full of water. "No rummy spoor here. But we'll find them."

Don sneezes.

"Enjoying the hunt?" Papa asks sardonically.

"I'm an indoor person."

"You haven't had the right exposure. More than once Blixen and I drove a hundred miles in a day and were never out of sight of the herds. Tommies, kudu, Grant's gazelle. They go to the rains, which were falling always just out of reach, to the north, to the west. The five senses of man are not enough to appreciate this beauty, a million antelope but space for a million more, or ten million. The lions followed the herds, and we followed the lions. Leopard too. The most difficult of all to kill, if you kill fairly and not by blinding them with lights where they come to feed or drink. They are truly cunning and dangerous because they hunt often in the dark and they themselves are darkness, except for the eyes, which are the true yellow color of a freshly cut key lime."

Don says crossly, "I don't know what that has to do with—"

"It has everything to do with becoming a hunter, which is now more than your obligation; you and your beauty may survive only if you hunt carefully and well. But Axman is the quickest of quarry, and no one has hunted him successfully before. Tell me all you know about him."

"There's not much to tell. If it was the same man, then—he may have killed as many as twenty-five people over a two-year period in four Midwestern states. I did some research after I knew I was in love with Shannon. I took time off and went out there, talked to the police and read all the accounts of the murders I could find. The Cobb family in Briarwood, Missouri. The Hanyards in Crestview, Iowa. The De La Warrs in Hendricks, Nebraska. And Shannon's family. September 1962 to June of 1964. There are similarities in each case. Five members in each family, although in Briarwood an au pair girl was also a victim. A fifteen- or sixteen-year-old daughter in each household. Blond. He chose families that had only a few or no pets, except for the De La Warrs, who raised golden retrievers. But they were in a kennel away from the house. From the variety and type of wounds the FBI concluded he used the same weapon over and over, an ax with a curved blade or blades that he kept razor-sharp. He left an old whetstone in the Cobb house that couldn't be traced. There was a partial footprint in new carpeting at the Hanyards'. From that the experts concluded he wore bowling shoes, was about six-one and weighed between one hundred seventy and one hundred eighty pounds. They were also able to tell he was right-handed. Scores of relatives of the four families were questioned, but no links between any of the victims could be established. Apparently they were chosen at random. The Axman left the same message, scrawled in blood on a variety of surfaces with paint brushes he found: 'I like to chop.'

"He, ah, apparently had no bias toward any particular part of the anatomy. He often dismembered victims after they were dead. He did not sexually molest males or females, not in a conventional or detectable manner. He liked to string the bodies up, usually in the cellars, by hammering cement nails into the walls. He used wire, clothesline, fishing line. A flute belonging to Timmie Cobb, one of three girls in the Briarwood case, was found next to her severed head. She'd been a flautist in her school band. He left no fingerprints; at least no prints recurred in the four houses he visited. There . . . isn't much else. Shannon survived. Untouched, by the merest stroke of good luck; or, perhaps, it had nothing to do with luck. The boy died before he could speak, so the police never knew what part he may have played in her escape. It's possible he knew the Axman, although they later ruled out the possibility he may have been an accomplice. Unmatched blood samples were found on his knife in the Hill house. The Axman, who obviously was injured, got away, only to die in some place where his remains are undiscovered. But that's speculation, based on the fact that the murders stopped; his *modus operandi* was not repeated after the massacre in Emerson."

"And what has your beauty had to say about her experiences with Axman?"

"Whatever she knows, she's stuck it away in a place with a lot of cobwebs. Shan managed to survive, mentally and emotionally, for four years after the massacre by literally denying her own identity, inventing a different background for herself. Her case has been exhaustively written up in psychiatric journals. She created, in comic-strip format— there are thousands of panels—another family of which she was a member, a fictitious but wholly safe environment in which to live. The Tafts of Roseboro, Kansas. The team that treated her at the psychiatric clinic found her artistic imagination very helpful in affecting a reintegration of her shattered personality. When she no longer needed 'Suzy Taft,' Shannon wrote her out of the strip, so to speak. Just as the other Tafts—mother, father, 'Suzy's' two brothers—died, nonviolently, and were buried as she came to grips with what really happened to her family.''

"Axman was never in the strip. But she's used the same means to try to get rid of him.''

"Yes. She certainly tried. But she couldn't draw him. It was frustrating for her. 'If I could get him right,' Shan told me, 'he'll disappear forever.' But who knows if she ever saw his face? He struck in the dead of night, when they—the families—were most vulnerable. Oh, God. Some of her efforts were—disgusting, horrifying. Inhuman. The closer we came to our wedding day, the more compelled she was to draw. She was making a—a terrible effort to purge him, to be free and happy. I felt so sorry. There was nothing I could do to help her.''

"I believe she has never wanted to see, to draw him truly. Because the consequences were bound to be the reverse of what she hoped she would achieve. Your beauty's creative imagination is a force beyond her control. Her pain is deep. Axman's evil is an image of that pain, which he gave to her. Now Axman has trapped her, in circumstances she has always feared. He is exhausting her in order to seduce her. He has the means. Her only defense is to draw—anything, everything that comes to mind but him."

"She drew *you*, didn't she? She imagines, it's real, like *that*. I had a little taste of what she can do, once, just a taste, and I—put it out of my mind and got damned good and shit-faced in a hurry, because what was the alternative? Believing the unbelievable? Damn it, I have *no* imagination myself, I never have nightmares, for Christ's sake I—"

"Carnes!"

"What?"

"We have both been drawn," Papa says, frowning. "That will be our greatest danger, as hunters."

"What hunters? We can't even get inside this fucking building! We need crowbars and axes, a rescue squad. I'm going to—"

Papa sniffed twice, alertly.

"Rummy spoor. This is where it is."

"Where what is? You want to know, my experience with Shannon's imagination? Not counting tonight—what with "Man of the Year" honors and then, poof! it's all gone in a cloud of hellfire—tonight's certainly been a pip, but the other time, after we met and . . . and we started making love. One afternoon we did it three times, I've never had orgasms like that before or since. They were the Old Faithful, the Niagara, the Hiroshima of orgasms. But I wasn't tired afterward, I felt— tremendous. Maybe a little, um, dazed, but in a wonderful way. Cheerful and happier than I'd ever thought I could be, just so . . . full of loving. Shan was sitting naked on the window seat in the bedroom, drawing. I asked her what it was and she showed it to me: a cute little bird like those you used to see fluttering around in the old Disney movies when Cinderella or Snow White was down in the dumps.

"She said, 'Watch, Donnie,' and pursed her lips in kind of a funny way, rubbed her fingers and thumb on the pencil she'd been drawing with, and the goddam bird flew right off the paper. Shannon looked at me with big dreamy eyes blue as lakes and that's when I felt, hell, like a kid back when I was growing up in Oswego and a wave of Lake Ontario would come barreling in over me; it wasn't any kind of trick, though, she hadn't dragged the bird in from the window ledge feeder just to fool me—I'm telling you truthfully, Papa, *right off the damn paper*! Shannon just smiled as it circled around the bedroom, a real

169

honest-to-God bird, and not at all panicky like birds indoors get. Pretty little bluebird. The bluebird of happiness?" Don honks twice into his soppy handkerchief. "Are you listening to me, Papa?"

"No. I'll need you to give me some help here."

Papa has one foot up on a narrow ledge about three feet above the sidewalk. He is sliding the fingers of his left hand along the margin of a handbill pasted over a rectangle of plywood; suddenly his fingers disappear as if sliced off by a guillotine.

Papa grunts, satisfied. "Thought so." He raises his other hand to pull at the plywood. There is some give in it, a sound of rusty hinges, a narrow space evident despite the dark and the rain.

"Pull!" Papa says, and Don lends his own strength to enlarging the space.

"There was a door here once—little wider—okay, I'll hold it while you step inside. Watch where you put your feet."

Don, prudently, cranes to try to see into the building before offering his body to it. The building breathes damply into his face: a tomblike miasma. He shudders.

"Without a light, maybe we shouldn't—owwww!"

Don goes sprawling inside from the

force of Papa's foot on his backside. He picks himself up off a floor littered with, among other things, sawdust and bits of broken glass. Damn lucky he wasn't cut. He is smarting from indignation. He'd read somewhere that the famous author could be a bully. Skitterings in the dark, and Don turns lumpishly cold: mice, or, worse, rats. He reaches up to reset his glasses, which are near the end of his nose, shudders again and sneezes. He hears paper tearing. A car goes by in the street and in the narrow space of the doorsill he sees a lit-up Papa, salt-and-pepper whiskers glowing like a Halloween cat. He is ripping a couple of old handbills from the street side of the plywood.

"What are you up to?"

Papa props the heavy rectangle of plywood open with an elbow and twists the strips of handbills tightly together.

"Those won't burn. Aren't they wet?"

"A little damp. But plenty of glue for fuel. Two of these will give us a good light. Fifteen, twenty minutes' worth."

Papa tosses one of the makeshift torches down to Don.

"Hold this."

Don looks away, toward the vague and shadowy flickering.

"Smoke," Papa says, his nose still working much better than Don's. "Rummies would have a fire on a night like this." He has taken matches from a pocket beneath his sou'wester. Strikes one and gets the end of his improvised torch glowing. Hands it down to Don. "We don't want it to burn too fast," he advises. He climbs down from the ledge, letting the hinged plywood settle into place behind him.

Don looks around the floor, which is concrete. The former department store was evidently stripped to the bare walls and cleaned out in advance of renovation that has never occurred. The smouldering torch affords just enough light to see a few feet into the blackness, enabling them to avoid pillars or pitfalls. Where are the elevators? He tries to remember how they went in and out on his only visit to Knightsbridge Publishers, the occasion a cocktail party honoring Shannon when one of her ten books for children reached the hundred-thousand copy mark in sales.

"At one time there were elevators and escalators in the store," he says to Papa. "But the only elevator left was the one they used while they were doing construction work on the upper floors. That has to be the elevator Shannon's in."

172

"No use to us if it's stuck up there between floors. What about stairs?"

"I don't know; there must be a stairway. We'll just have to look around until we—*God in heaven, what was that?*"

Startled by the echoing, flattened trumpet call, Don takes a step back on the floor littered with scraps of paper, old bones and copious black droppings, jostling Papa, who keeps his own footing and lifts his head eagerly. They hear it again, eerie, reverberating, and this time a look of almost reverential joy appears in the old hunter's eyes, he smiles from ear to ear.

"That," Papa says, "is a fornicating elephant. Looks like I've come home again."

Home.

To Perry Kennold, home is an Airstream trailer, far from new when his old man acquired it for a little cash, an eighteen-foot speedboat with dry rot where it didn't show and a Mercury outboard that had a bent propeller shaft, also something not at all obvious until you tried to rev it over ten miles an hour. For eight years he has lived in the Airstream in six different states, never far down a dusty road from one vast construction site or another. Lived with his brawling parents and his little sister, who finally fled at the age of fourteen with a bowlegged half-Crow son of a sugarbeet farmer from Harding, Montana. He's had three postcards from Elsie since then, the last from somewhere up in Alberta, Canada, where she was a waitress and her husband was working off six weeks for disorderly conduct and public drunkenness. The good news is, she still isn't pregnant; the bad news is, she has acne too, not as bad as Perry's but as she described her condition, her cheeks look like blueberry muffins.

Perry misses Elsie and she said she missed him too; but he realizes it is no good asking her to come back, at least not until he is making his own way in the world and has a place for her to stay. When she was eleven or twelve their father had begun taking too much of an interest in Elsie, though he only became real aggressive when he was drunk, and then he couldn't do much, because of how the booze affected him, except with his middle finger. But that was bad enough. It all but killed Elsie's spirit and her sense of humor, and although she would never admit everything to Perry, he knew, and was depressed and afraid, afraid because he couldn't sleep some nights for thinking what it would be like to put a knife in his father's heart. Anyway, Elsie solved their mutual dilemma by eloping, and things improved between Perry and the old man, particularly when Perry put on nearly twenty-five pounds of muscle one summer and, after his father insisted on Indian-wrestling, wrenched his neck badly.

In the trailer Perry sleeps, as he's always done, on a built-in couch in the larger cabin a few feet away from the vibrating refrigerator and the dripping faucet in the little sink. The interior is pretty much a shambles: a film of grease everywhere from smoky fry-pans, worn-out carpet and upholstery with big chunks missing, as if gnawed on; two windows cracked, venetian blind slats fly-specked and bent. His father sleeps in back, in the only bedroom, and since he broke his tibia and cracked the patella of his left knee he spends a lot of time on the bed in a midthigh cast watching daytime TV, adding to his beer belly and complaining about his rotten luck.

There are few grace notes in Perry's life;

his infatuation with Walt Whitman's poetry is one. (*The pleasures of heaven are with me, and the pains of hell are with me.*) His infatuation with Shannon Hill is another.

Perry has several photos of Shannon. Four of these are in the high-school yearbook, the *Road Runner*, including her junior class portrait, which is only one inch by two inches and in black-and-white. Not his favorite, because it emphasizes a certain vapid thinness of mouth, a prematurely spinsterish look that he doesn't notice when talking to her. His favorite photo is one he swiped, peeling it off a poster in school one afternoon after lingering until he was sure the halls were empty. Shannon, cochairman of the junior prom committee. Her head is up and she's laughing in this candid color shot (*This head more than churches, bibles, and all the creeds*). He carries the purloined photo in his wallet, carefully wrapped in several thicknesses of tissue paper so it can't be sweat-stained or scratched.

Everybody must have noticed the photo was missing and probably some of Shannon's friends teased her about it. If she had her suspicions as to who took it, she didn't let on in biology, the one class they shared during the day, or in the halls where he contrived as often as possible to run into Shannon between classes. He allowed himself to believe that Shannon not only knew he had the picture, but approved. It was a comfortable secret they shared, dearer to him than words. Her usual greeting, as she came swirling down the hall with an armload of books, was a quick smile and sometimes a shrug, excusing herself: "Busy, busy, busy." He knew how busy and active she was. Prom committee, newspaper, student council (recording secretary, junior class). Art Club. Girl's volleyball. He was proud of Shannon. He could even manage without a twinge of jealousy when he saw her with other guys: the senior-class president she sometimes dated, the jocks. None of them as big as Perry; he took comfort in that, even though he had no athletic ability. But the football teams always needed beef in the line, so maybe next year—

Perry's alarm goes off at four-thirty A.M. He wakes up with a skipped heart beat and shortness of breath, something that happens to him from time to time, particularly after a wet dream. The fly front of the Jockey briefs he slept in is stiff from his emission. But like always, coming in his sleep hasn't afforded total satisfaction.

Yearningly he turns over on the narrow couch and embraces a pillow. There is a rooster crowing somewhere, a dog barking. His first waking thoughts are of Shannon. He reaches into his shorts. The air in the trailer is stale. He is sweaty all over. In the dark he squeezes himself almost painfully, squeezes again. (*The mystic amorous night, the strange half-welcome pangs*). He tries to imagine her asleep, beside him, then drowsily opening her eyes. Smiling at him. (*O you and me at last, and us two only*). Ohh, God! But it's going to take too much time, young as he is. He has to be at work at five-thirty, out on the Interstate bypass. They're pouring today. Saturday, time-and-a-half, he and his father need the money.

Perry gets up and peels himself out of the soiled underwear. He finds another pair in one of the drawers built into the underside of the couch and carries the shorts into the bathroom, which he has to enter at an angle because of the width of his shoulders; the doorway is only about a foot and a half wide. He uses the toilet and splashes his face with water, takes inventory. Traces of brownish Clearasil above his eyebrows, on his cheeks. No better or worse than yesterday. The dermatologist in town says he won't scar much, if at all, just wait it out, Perry. There's a new one on his chin by the deep cleft and he attacks almost savagely, punishing the zit until the core is out and the hole that remains fills with fresh blood. He blots it, applies more Clearasil everywhere and stares at himself in the bleak mirror, feeling cast down and afflicted, even though his day has barely started.

He'll drive by her house before going to work.

O you whom I often and silently come where you are that I may be with you . . .

Just the thought of driving down West Homestead before the crack of dawn, pulling over in front of Shannon's house and looking up at the windows where he thinks her bedroom is (last two windows on the left, second floor), and where he has seen her, twice, at night, in silhouette against the drawn shades and flimsy curtains, the thought is sufficient to revive and fill him with an electric anticipation, the mainspring of certain and desirable Fate winding ever-tighter in his breast.

He wears frayed jeans and a T-shirt to work, taking along his denim vest because it will be chilly out on the road until an hour after dawn. He munches handfuls of dried Wheaties, washes them down with bottled orange juice, then makes his lunch. Six slices of bologna and a lot of mayonnaise on white bread, two Hostess cupcakes (needs the ener-

179

gy, although he knows the sugar will add fuel to all the little volcanoes on his face and neck and shoulders), pours a quart of milk into a thermos. He attaches his Buck knife in its scabbard to his belt. No trouble yet with the guys he works with, but he has been in a lot of fights and knows the value of intimidation—a scowl, his big shoulders, the plainly visible Buck knife, which, opened, has a five-inch blade.

Four forty-five. His father is snoring. When he's awake he has trouble getting around with the cast on his leg, and twice has spilled the can he pees and expectorates in at night, trying to get it to the sink to empty it. Adding to the general squalor and disagreeableness of their cramped living space. Perry thinks maybe he ought to go in there and attend to this bothersome chore, but the old man probably will wake up and think of six other things Perry needs to do before he takes off for work. Hell with that. Truck keys in a pocket of his fleece-lined vest, a coming-apart paperback edition of *Leaves of Grass* in another. He leaves the Airstream quietly, not rocking it much with his weight as he steps out and takes a slow look around.

More than one rooster is stirring in semirural coops across the willow-lined river from the trailer park. Stars still visible directly overhead but the sky is lightening eastward. Some lights on in the mobile homes around him. A collicky baby screaming, probably the same baby he heard just before falling asleep, nine hours ago. The bad news is they cry a lot. But the good news is they don't stay babies for long. Before you know it they're three or four years old, and kids can be a lot of fun. Perry has gazed at a pearl of semen on his fingertip and thought of how many babies it would make. Flunked biology through sheer lack of interest, but he learned this much: one drop of the fun stuff, a thousand babies. Ten thousand. But one baby will be enough for him— his baby. Shannon's. He gets into the GMC truck, carelessly knocking an elbow in his mooniness, wondering what her stuff looks like, tastes like. His only sexual experience with a thirty-five-year-old woman he babysat for in New Mexico. Three kids, the oldest three-and-a-half. Aroma of fried food in her hair, on her skin. In heat her secretions had a harsh odor, like soap with lye in it. Nipples tasting of dried mother's-milk. A wolfish sneer on her face as she came, straddling him, twisting down and down into his lap, getting hers with a vengeance. A little later, in a lull, she would teach him to go after her pussy as if he were sucking the juice from an orange. Breasts heaving, eyes way back in her head.

He hadn't really liked her but was excited by her excitement, her wild, red hair.

Now there was Shannon, skin cleanly shining, unblemished as a doll's. Shannon, virginal, will be different. Perry doesn't like to think about the possibility that she might have done it with somebody else already. No. He's sure. Girls who have done it have a different way of looking at you, their eyes sooner or later just go to your crotch. Shannon Hill is a virgin. Does she get crabby once a month, like Elsie did? Circles under her pretty eyes? He is going to see Shannon. What if, what if there's a chance he could just open the door of her house and tiptoe upstairs to where she sleeps and—. He aches. His genitals are hot as a toaster, he's swollen in his Levis, which makes it difficult and a little painful to drive. Her photo in his wallet. Would she like to go to a movie tonight? Is it too soon to be calling her? Please, please, go with me tonight, Shannon!

I have somewhere surely lived a life of joy with you

Two deaths have been improvised, and done as well as he could do them.

But this is the part the Axman likes best:

With the stately symphonic poem taking shape in his head (reminiscent of, but certainly not borrowed from, Siegfried's Funeral Music in the third act of *Die Götterdammerung*), he takes the time to again look around the master bedroom with his pencil flashlight. This time there are sleepers, whom he does not disturb but studies with what amounts to familial compassion as he waits for those moments in the course of the threnody that are certain to move him to tears: waits to lead them in their unmarriage vows, to unjoin them in holy bloodletting.

(If one should wake, and if one could see in the dark, and had chilling moments of apprehension, of realization, then one would see a yellow hard hat, and beneath its narrow brim clear polycarbonate goggles already besmirched, little pinpoints of quick-dry bloodspatter. One would see the unblinking unwavering eyes of a curious man. Yes, curious, not inimical, nor gloating, nor wishing the sleepers pain, which is the beauty of the heavy ax he holds, no bone a barrier to the sharpness of the blades he carefully hones after every third or fourth stroke, circumstances permitting. He is respectful of his victims, aware of the very great privilege they

183

afford him in the drawing of their blood. He wishes they all could hear the music, but that's the rub: the music is of their dying, during their dying; no one will hear the full symphony except she who he has chosen to be the last, *his* gift to her fine, unblemished soul.)

The beam of the penlight moves with the silence of a butterfly over surfaces, is reflected in its poignant searching from mirrors, glassware, the screen of a bulky TV set, rabbit ears wrapped in crinkly aluminum foil. As he looks, he moves, never more than a step at a time, gradually coming ever-closer to the bed with the high birdseye-maple headboard, forming a scrolled crest a third of the way up the wall above which are positioned family photographs. Her family? His? Axman doesn't know. There is a thinness, a sallowness to the countryfolk in the group photos, not a smile to be spared, a certain dogged reluctance to look the camera in the eye. Churchyard. After a wedding, no doubt; who poses for photographs following a funeral? To a man they wear dark suits and fedoras; the women's flowered dresses reach to the top ankle strap of their best shoes. 1930's, even earlier, to judge from vintage high-roofed automobiles parked in the background.

The
 beam
 traces
down the papered wall, the headboard, steadies there as a sleeper shifts beneath the quilt,
breaks wind obliviously. He waits, agreeably
chilled by the recurrence of the *leitmotiv*
conceived so effortlessly at the first fall of his
ax downstairs. He listens intently, but there is
nothing in the music he would change. Impatient to get on with what he is creating—but
this is the inevitable lull before the next
gorgeous, incredible gush of inspiration. As
the music begins to fade from his mind (not
losing it, no, it is always there even though he
must sometimes shift his concentration outside himself, as if taking a short stroll away
from the concert hall), he lets the light play on
the wiry unkempt head and freckled brow of
Ernestine Hill. Her eyelids shiny, purplish
ovals. She is lying on her stomach, breathing
through slack lips. One bare arm is thrown
over the side of the bed, fingers trailing on the
floor near where an ashtray, matches, a packet
of cigarette papers and sack of tobacco are
piled on top of a seed catalogue. Very small
diamond in the wedding band which in turn is
deep in the flesh below an enlarged, obstruc-
tive knuckle. She is wearing some kind of

corset-thing beneath her flimsy sleeveless nightgown. Maybe it's for her back. One other problem, the sheet and quilt, though folded back and covering the sleepers only to about their waists, are still in the way. He has to remove them. But first a look at Dab, face-up and snoring less than two feet apart from his wife. Undershirt and skivvies. One knee raised. He moves the light across Dab, back to Ernestine, again to Dab from tattooed arm to hairy shoulders, all the while approaching the bed. The light in his left hand. The ax in his right, at his side, the bit swinging in a short arc just off the floor. Which squeaks under his weight. Not much of a noise, but in the bed Dabney Hill breaks off in mid-snore, jerks, mumbles. Instantly the light is off.

He waits, two or three minutes, for Dab to adjust himself on the mattress, breathe deeply, commence snoring again. The light.

flick

/////////////////////////

Dab is still on his back,
nostrils high, mouth
open, adam's apple like

a hut of cartilage on the
exposed
throat.

flick a vacan-
cy
////////////////////

in Dab's mouth, he re-
moved
a partial upper bridge
before retiring.

                    flick

again, back to the
throat. Lingering //////////
there, pale
as a moonbeam. So.
                    Dab
will be the first, and headless, even as
Ernestine dreams on with furrowed brow and
twisted lip.
    Dearly beloved how I adore you for the
blood you dedicate to me
    His devotional all but inaudible as the
music thunders through his head.
    The light is out.
    In the dark he pulls down the quilt on

the bed, slowly, until they both lie uncovered, unknowing.

Exultant, the Axman weeps.

Awake, Shannon?

Someone is calling her by that name again.

Not one of the psych-techs. It has to be a newcomer on the floor, but whoever it is, he should know better. She will not respond to that name. If he doesn't know what to correctly call her, she will go on lying there with her eyes closed, on the narrow bed. Face to the unadorned, pastel-yellow concrete block wall. Her knees drawn up, hands clasped between her thighs. The position she finds most comfortable . . . endurable is more like it. She can go on for long stretches at a time like this, ignoring the body's most basic demands. Thirst. Hunger. Meaningless. Lying in shit. Meaningless. Blood—but she has no blood. Her veins, arteries, empty, waxen. Her heart contracting, expanding rhythmically, but the chambers are scoured clean. Total emptiness. No blood.

Now leave me alone.

You can't get away from me that easily, Shannon.

Oh, she'd like to teach him a lesson! But, ironclad rule, she *never* talks to strangers, those who have mistaken her for someone else. Is this Georgia's day off? She will not move or blink until Georgia comes around and greets her properly, warm and chuckling: "Well, how are we feelin' today, Suzylamb? Oh, oh, did we have a little accident while we was snug asleep? Don't you worry about that, sugar, have it cleaned right up." She loves Georgia. And Dr. McLarty, the whimsical Irishman with the awful pipe tobacco and plaid vests, hair too thin and lazy to comb, eyes big as a squid's behind thick glasses: she loves him, too. "I like the new strip. What a

189

problem! That stray puppy Suzy brought home chewed a hole in mom's favorite sofa cushion." "Suzy'll patch it, and mom will never notice." "Then she'll get to keep the puppy?" "Oh, sure. A family needs a puppy." "He might get into more mischief, though. He might do something really bad." "No, he *won't*. See, he's sorry about the sofa cushion, and he'll never do a thing like that again. He loves Suzy, because she gave him a home." "Tell me something—" Dr. Firmikin speaking; he wears glasses too—but with severe, dark frames. She doesn't love Dr. Firmikin. He seldom says anything, but when he asks her a question, the question frequently makes her nervous, uneasy. Then when she replies he'll rub his temple with the eraser of a pencil as if perplexed, not pleased with her answer. "Why does Suzy like dogs better than cats?" Always that kind of question: difficult. But for this one she has an answer she doesn't have to prepare. "Cats are too quiet. They prowl around at night. They have—" "Claws?" *No, no, guess again. But I'm not talking. I'll never tell.*

Shannon, get up. You've made a mess. You have to clean yourself.

*Georgia, you do it for me? Please? I'm sorrrryyy. I've been **SO** good; haven't done it in my sleep for months and months.*

I'm not Georgia. And you're a long way from the hatch in Topeka. But we've all been wondering, when are you going to finish the strip? Make a few important changes. Draw the truth, this time.

"Where am I?"

You're in the elevator.

(In the elevator. And oh God, it is so dark! At the clinic the light, at her request, was always on, that first eighteen months. Between bouts of torpor, indifference, she would swing to new highs of creative activity, drawing, drawing, until her fingers ached or trembled and she could no longer hold the crayons they allowed her to have. At first, until she was accustomed to crayons, she had to

191

draw clumsily, on a big scale. Suzy. Mom. Pop. Richie. David. The Tafts of Roseboro, Kansas. Removed in recent years to a distant asterism of the mind.

She had almost forgotten what they looked like although—she knows—wherever they are, they still smile a lot. Mom wore pearls and good-looking blouses around the Colonial-style house, and Pop always had a tie on with his cardigan sweater. She never knew what he did for a living. There were always flowers in the Tafts' foyer. Richie delivered papers on his motorscooter and Dave went to law school at the college in town, but he often found time to play basketball with his little brother in the driveway. Suzy's bedroom had a four-poster canopy bed. A double-sized walk-in closet filled with the nice things she bought from the money she made babysitting and doing chalk portraits at the county fair. She didn't slip and mess her pants when she was terrified and lonely. Suzy Taft was never terrified and lonely. But Shannon Hill—

(She groans as she moves on the gritty elevator floor. The floor seems unsteady to her and she is reminded, horridly, of being in suspension—just how, she doesn't know, something to do with wheels and cables—in a high rectangular shaft. How high? The elevator scarcely seemed to have started down before the lights, two ordinary dusty bulbs in wire cages on the ceiling and well out of her reach even if she stood on tiptoe, failed to a deathlike brownish-yellow and the apparatus jolted to a stop. She freezes, listening. Thinks she hears a soft tapping or dripping overhead. Water. Rain on the roof of the building that has found a way into the elevator shaft. Again she moves, a hand against the wall behind her. Almost trips over her shoulder bag and portfolio, the thick drawing pad that goes everywhere with her. A pencil rolls. She had been drawing, in the dark. But now her lower back aches, her head aches, her throat is dry. And she can smell herself.

(Shannon unbuckles and lowers her pleated, men's-style trousers. Takes them off. Then the panties. It isn't too bad. She wads the panties and throws them away from her, takes tissue from her purse. When she feels clean and decent again she dresses. She can hear herself breathing. That, and a slow drip of leaking rain. The cold sound sets her to shivering, ferociously. How long has she been trapped? Her head pounds, hard to think. Should she yell again, scream, try to get someone's attention? Anyone else but *him*—

(Who is, uncharacteristically, quiet now.

(Somehow she doesn't feel abandoned. No.

(Which means something important has happened, to alter the delicate balance of their relationship.

(She places her hands over her face, feels the lids of her eyes, tight as rosebuds in the darkness; they will open only to the sun. It occurs to her that she may have had her eyes closed from the moment the lights went out. Seeing all that she cared to see within protectively sealed lids. Sketching in darkness by the mind's brilliant eye.

(If she should open them now, and look around her—

(*Nothing to be afraid of.* But the reassurance is almost too quick—glib, seductive. Not her thought, but his.

(Something *happened*. More than her bowels slipped while she was sprawled, insensibly, on the elevator floor.

(Look. What harm can there be in looking? The lights may have come on.

(No. I'm blind. I **want** to be blind. I want my eyes, my brain, to be as empty of vision as my veins are empty of blood.

(**Do you understand?** I have no blood. No sight. I'm worthless to you. Go away, forever!)

Silence.

. . . Music.

No! I will be deaf, too! I will not hear your damned music!

(Oh, too late. She has not prepared, she cannot shut out the symphonic torrent.

(Turning, she hammers both fists against the elevator wall. The elevator shudders and she knows she has miscalculated: wheels, cables, brakes, they have no strength to resist the force of her terror; she must fall.

(Unless, in this instant of her undoing, she can go to sleep again.

(But where will she wake up *next* time?)

In her own bed, of course.

Saturday, June the sixth, 1964.

It is now four minutes after five in the morning, and no longer quite dark out there. The city birds are awake and thriving: bush-dwelling prairie warblers that live in the tall lilac by the side of the garage, the tinny-sounding nuthatches, chattering wrens, genial robins.

Shannon sighs deeply, then rolls to her right toward the center of the bed but does not, as she expects, come up against Chapman's warm boyish body. Someone to hug and hold against her breast as she has done since he was very little. Some day, perhaps this year, she will no longer be able to sleep with him; that special innocence will be lacking and they both will know it. Just as she, with the onset of menstruation, had felt wrong about creeping into Allen Ray's bed those nights when she craved his brotherly protection.

The lightness of her bed, the absence of Chap's raspy breath, lifts her a little above the surface of sweet oblivion, and she makes another sound in her throat, moistens her lips with her tongue. Her eyelids twitch and she tugs at the top of her pajamas, which are twisted and putting pressure on her sore breasts. Shannon thinks Chap must have gone back to his own room when the birds began to stir and forage. But her little brother is not in his room. Nor is he asleep. And she is the last one left.

The narrow beam of a pencil flashlight touches one shoulder, her charmingly bent earlobe. Lingers there. Vanishes. Reappears on her smooth forehead. Illuminates a high round cheekbone. Grazes, caresses.

She is lying on her back.

Her eyes open suddenly.

"*What*?"

"Don't be afraid," he whispers from the darkness. "It's me."

Sitting up quickly, recognizing his voice, thrilled but knowing he shouldn't be there, in her bedroom: my God what *is* he doing there, or did he tell when he called yesterday that he was coming by this early? Did they make a date for breakfast, has she overslept? No, that couldn't be it, something must be wrong, he needs her. *An accident*, she thinks. He's had an accident, his plane—*he's hurt*—

"Rob," Shannon says quietly, though her heart is stuffing blood at an unmanageable rate through her throat to her brain, "just a minute. I'll get up. Let me turn on the light."

Perry Kennold knows he's going to be late for work, but he can't help himself. No willpower. He just can't turn the key in the ignition, put the truck in gear, drive away from Shannon's house without giving it his best shot.

This hour I tell things in confidence,
I might not tell everybody, but I will tell
you.

He has a notebook on him, in which he sometimes jots down his thoughts, observations in poesy. What he'd like to do now is ask her for a date, but in a way that will cause her to take some notice of him, alert her to the fact that he's not just another guy with a bad complexion and no future. He has deep feelings about life. He wants the note to be amusing, clever, sensitive. So she will read it and think, This is the real Perry. *I'd love to go out with you; why didn't you ask me sooner?*

He finds a clean page at the back of the pocket notebook, and a pencil stub in the dashboard compartment of the pickup. He uses his right knee for a writing desk, and has enough light from the glow of the instrument panel. The clock reading four-and-a-half minutes after five. He hears a distant rooster. A car goes by up the block, crossing West Homestead. The truck's radio is on, tuned very low, to Patsy Cline.

Dear Shannon:

Another minute goes by.

His eyes begin to burn from concentrating on the paper, his face is stiff and dry. Too much Clearasil. He glances up at her windows, yearning for inspiration. A lamp goes on; his heart lights up as well. Past the leaf-pattern darkness of a tree there is an interior shadow on a window shade; he recognizes her. The shape of her head, the distinctive ducky haircut. Then another shadow, unexpected, swift, overtaking, overwhelming her; the shadows merge, the light flares as if the lampshade has been knocked off. Perry leans toward the window on the curb-side trying to see better, but the lamp, apparently, is on the floor. Then it's off again, just as one of the window shades is disturbed and goes flying up. He has a blurred impression of something pale, like a bare foot, near the glass. But nothing more.

Perry opens the door and gets out, disturbed, tingling all over. He sees somebody there in her bedroom, briefly, as the shade is lowered. Just a torso, an arm—a dark, perhaps gloved, hand.

He goes running up the walk to the porch, boots clumping heavily on the floorboards. There has to be a doorbell, but he can't find it. The screen door isn't latched. The front door is not locked. Perry barges right in.

"Shannon!"

His mind is boiling, his heart lurching as if crippled by terror. His voice does not come out too strong. Almost a croak. He swallows, a foot on the first step of the stairway, calls again. Wake them all up, who cares? Something's not right here.

"Shannon, it's Perry!"

"Who?" A cross and sleepy voice, not Shannon's. From the top of the stairs. He can't see who's up there. "What are you doing here?"

"I'm a friend of Shannon's. I was just driving by. I saw—somebody was in her room. Who are you?"

"Allen Ray. Shannon's brother." His voice down to a whisper. "Shannon had a— nightmare. I put her back to bed. You'd better get out of here. I've got a gun in my room. So does my dad. You don't want to wake *him* up."

Perry, suddenly not so sure of anything, takes his foot off the step. The sudden drop of blood from his overloaded brain leaves him dazed. He can't believe he's made a mistake, done something really stupid like this. But—

"Is she awake? Could I—"

"Keep your voice down." He's angry. "If you don't get out of here right now you're going to be in trouble. A lot of trouble."

"All I want is to be sure—"

A heavy sigh. "I suppose I'm not going to get rid of you that easy, am I?"

"I have to go to work. I'm late now." Shannon must have heard him, Perry thinks. She couldn't have gone back to sleep in the half-minute since he ran up to the house. Unless she was sleepwalking to begin with. Maybe that was it. The only thing to do is apologize, turn around and walk out—

"You've really interfered. Now I've lost it. The entire score. I have to start over. I hope you're satisfied. Whatever your name is."

"Perry. I'm sorry." Interfered? What score? Allen Ray sounds a little weird. Not like an ex-jock who works in a garage, races cars for a hobby. "Look, I'm going. Maybe you better not tell Shannon about this. It was just a mistake."

"Come up and tell her yourself. She's not asleep. I'm going back to bed."

"Come up—?"

"I said it was okay, didn't I? I'll turn on the light for you." Perry hears the creak of flooring. "Damn. It's out. Come on anyway. I'll turn the lamp on in her room."

He hears Allen Ray walking in the hall

upstairs. The stairs are dark, beyond the first two. He puts a hand on the railing and starts up, slowly. Not sure it is the right thing to do. He'll have to invent some good reason why he'd been passing by her house at this hour—oh, the hell with it, Perry thinks. Just tell her how he feels, get it over with. This recklessness excites him, scares him. He moves more quickly up the stairs, ten, twelve of them, but still he can't see, there's no light anywhere. Allen Ray seems to have vanished. Perry knows he's in a forbidden place at the wrong hour: it's eerie, not unlike some dreams he's had, but he can't stop himself.

The top step. Which way? He looks around the corner to his left and there's a streak of light shining through a doorway down the hall, he can see green leaves with brown tips in a planter. *Your brother said you wouldn't mind if I just said hello. I've got to get to work—you know, out on the Interstate. Maybe I'll see you tonight, if that's okay. Better get back to sleep now. ("Little you know the subtle electric fire that for your sake is playing within me.")*

At her door, which is half-closed.

"Shannon?"

He hears something. Not a word. Like a groan. Maybe telling him to come in. He pushes the door open, smiling sheepishly. The reading light clamped to the wrought-iron headboard is pointed at him. Hits him right in the eyes. The bed quakes. He sees her frantic tied-together hands and flailing feet. Then her face. Red from strangulation, the blue eyes watery, fathoms of terror. There's a rope around her neck, tied to the headboard. A patch of shiny silver-gray duct tape across her mouth.

She—

This isn't—

It can't—

"Oh, my." He hears the high-pitched voice behind him. "I thought you'd have your dick out by now, ready to f—"

Perry can't turn around quickly enough. Something hits him stunningly in the back, the left shoulder blade, and he is driven headfirst into the brass planter and bowl that contains a fat rubber plant. The ax blade is wrenched free of the shallow bone it lodged in, the ax comes slashing again with hardly a pause, blade clanging off the planter and ricocheting at a deep angle into the bicep of his left arm. He knows he's grievously hurt; the arm just hangs, blood flowing. Perry gets his feet under him quickly. Sensing certain death behind him, instinctively he doesn't turn around. The next swing of the ax is off the mark, missing him, blade striking the wall an inch from the back of his head. He tumbles

through the doorway into the master bedroom.

On his back, foot lashing out, he kicks
the door shut in the Axman's face. What little
he sees of that face in the backlighting from
Shannon's room is a terrifying sight: yellow
hard hat, clear goggles of the type construction men wear to protect their eyes from dust
and bits of rock and metal. A gauze mask
smeared with blood covers the nose and
mouth.

The ax rips into a panel of the stout
door, sticks momentarily; the Axman has to
work it free.

Perry sits up, fumbling for the Buck
knife on his belt.

"Shit!" In a frenzy to be after Perry, the
Axman kicks the door, kicks it again.

Perry puts the handle of the knife between his teeth and opens it with the fingers of
his right hand. On the left side, all numb, the
numbness spreading down his leg, scaring
him worse than the copious bleeding. The
madman with the ax now takes time to turn
the knob, open the door, step into the room.

Perry rolls frantically to his right onto
fringed carpeting. The ax thunders down like
the hammer of Thor into the carpet and
lodges solidly in the oak flooring. The Axman
must work it loose as Perry scrambles blindly

backward, pulls himself up again, slowly, at the foot of a four-poster bed in which lie sleepers. *But how can they be sleeping through this?* He feels a drip of something on his face and looks up to discover a partial answer: there is a severed head impaled at sort of a cocky angle on one of the bedposts. Then the Axman is on him again, swinging horizontally and cutting him two inches deep across the belly.

In shock already, he feels almost nothing. The Axman, half-turned away from Perry at the conclusion of his full-length swing, has his right foot twisted in the carpet. Perry reacts unthinkingly. Right hand shooting out, five-inch blade up, almost all of it slicing through the Axman's liver and into his lung. He hears a squeal of dismay. His weight has shifted to his left and his leg can't hold him. Perry falls, knife coming out of the Axman. Bad cramp in his stomach. He must do something. Crawl. *Under the bed*, he thinks. Where the ax can't find him. But it's too late. *Oh, Shannon. I love you.* But too late.

He is looking at the Axman. The mask, the oval, sucked-in dimples where the nostrils would be. The protective glasses, spotted, eyes rolling wildly behind the lenses. Could this be Shannon's brother? No. Something terrible has happened to Allen Ray, to them all. With his ax half-raised for a killing stroke, a shudder runs through the Axman and he cries out in pain, the sound muffled by the mask. He tries again. There is a bright red spot the size of a quarter where his mouth would be. Perry's vision swims. His own pain, suddenly, is immense—he has to cough, wetness in his throat; the cough is nearly enough to kill him. When he recovers he senses he is alone. Through tearing eyes he cannot see well—where has the Axman gone?

Perry has no fight left in him. He lets go of the knife in favor of holding himself where the pain is. Just at the belt line, the belt cut in two, his abdomen open, his fingers slip in. Now breathing is a problem, and his head is expanding with a buoyant gas. He can't think. But he remembers: Shannon, on her bed, thrashing, asphyxiating. Must find the knife he dropped. Feels on the floor for it. Ah. Go now to Shannon. Maybe too late already. Try. Can't. *Get up!*

Weeping, Perry gets to his feet. In a crouch, right arm tight across the waist, where his navel used to be. Light from her room coming across the hall and into this room. Walk? No way to walk. Just hobble. Bluntly, as a beggar with no toes. The rumpled carpet a hazard for his feet. Fall again, never get up. His left arm still there but he feels it swinging oddly, as if the bones are disconnected. Looking down he sees the steady drip of blood from his nerveless fingertips. So scared. He looks around at the four-poster bed. *Shapes of the using of axes.* And eyes high above him, half-opened, blandly terrifying in their eternal dreaminess. Where is Axman now? Where gone? Hurt bad? What if he has gone back to Shannon's room? Get moving. *Kill him.*

The Axman's not in Shannon's room. She isn't thrashing and twisting on the bed now but Perry can't see her well; the light's in his eyes and there's a fog everywhere. Perry's teeth chatter, he's very cold; and he can't hold himself in any longer, there's a pulpy mass he doesn't want to look at slipping down over his right forearm. When he has to let go to cut her loose—Perry sobs. What if she's dead? Suddenly he can't do it. He slumps down on the side of Shannon's bed, too weak to scream at the violence of the pain. The fog so bad now the light on the headboard barely shines through it.

He can let go, though. Sitting down he's not afraid he'll spill everything out where the ax ripped him.

Shannon?

Perry blinks, trying to see her. His teeth won't stop chattering. He's beginning to see other things, also dear to him: his mother, little Elsie. There in the fog. Scenes of childhood. All of it going by very fast, but he's enraptured, he almost forgets—

The mattress begins to move under him. He is kicked in the thigh. Shannon's bare foot. He leans toward the headboard and there she is, too, in the fog, neck tightly bound, eyes bulging horribly. He reaches out, the hand with the knife, just as a cramp hits him. His bloody hand falls on her face. She kicks him again. He wants to tell her to stop, but his mouth is full. Can't talk with his mouth full. Can't swallow either. Slides the hand up through her hair, must be careful, not cut her with the knife. Cut the rope. Clothesline. Easy to do any other time, but he can't manage now. Roaring in his ears. Waterfall. The Colorado River flooding through the Grand Canyon. Rapids of the Snake. He's been there. Seen them all. Peaceful days in a knock-about life. *Cut the rope*. But he's busy now, navigating, alone in his canoe on the foggy, turbulent river. Coughs. Blood all over both of them. Shannon dying, will you—cut—the

He's not aware of having done it. But she's sitting up beside him, eyes a few inches from his own. His blood on her face and in her hair. Sucking wind through her nose so violently the nostrils are pressed shut with each intake.

She doesn't recognize Perry. There is nothing in her eyes but terror. He thinks, *Hi, Shannon*, but with her bound hands she is shoving him aside, nowhere to go but down the rapids, his disappointment as heavy as the rock where his belly should be. Sinking in darkness while his angel flies.

But now I think there is no unreturn'd love,
*   the pay is certain, one way or another*

Five-twenty-one a.m.

Robert McLaren leaves the house by the front door.

He has taken off the surgical mask but holds a handkerchief to his mouth, dabbing at the blood that rises steadily to the tip of his tongue, his lips. In his left hand, away from the side where his pierced liver and lung are causing him considerable discomfort, he carries the heavy toolbag containing everything he brought with him to 298 West Homestead. The sky in the east is the color of mercury, tinged with old gold. There is a dark red oval on the gray coveralls where Perry's knife went in, but most of the damage is internal. His liver. Right lung penetrated but not collapsed. He walks slowly down the steps and out to the curb where a pickup truck is parked at an angle with one door open. He looks inside. The keys are in the ignition. He lifts his tool-bag with several inches of half-erect protruding ax handle into the bed of the truck, shuts the door, goes around to the driver's side and gets in. Starts the engine. Drives off. No rush, no telltale squealing of tires. Thirty-four seconds have elapsed.

Within a minute-and-a-half he is seven blocks away, pulling up behind the rental car he left on one of the busier commercial streets of Emerson, Kansas.

Robert waits while a station wagon pulling a trailered boat goes by in the opposite direction. Farther down the street a sixteen-wheeler is coming, blazing with lights. He doesn't care. He's feeling just the least bit woozy now, partly from lack of sleep, and the handkerchief he holds more or less constantly to his lips is filling with blood.

He gets out of the pickup, leaving the keys, takes the toolbag from the back, feeling the strain of lifting now. Carries the toolbag to the rental car, unlocks it, puts the toolbag on the floor on some newspapers he spread there earlier. Gets in behind the wheel but doesn't leave immediately, just stares east through the windshield where the sun will rise soon. He listens, hopefully, but he doesn't hear it.

I have to hear the music, Shannon. The music is the only thing that keeps me from going insane.

Where will he find another family in time?

He starts the car, makes a U-turn, and heads for the airport.

And as he drives he begins to sob, just crying his eyes out.

Madge Mayhew gets up early every morning to attend to her correspondence and other writings before her husband Adolphus, a retired lawyer, starts bumbling around in the bathroom and then the kitchen, disturbing her. Madge writes an average of thirty letters per week; some of them run to a dozen pages. She's a genealogy buff, and for the last fourteen years has been working on a family history. The Hockenhulls. She's a vice-regent of the Magna Carta Dames and a fellow of the Colonial Order of the Crown, made up of lineal descendents of the Emperor Charlemagne. Pretty impressive. Madge compensates for the rather dull life she has lived with the man of her dreams, who can only trace his forbears back two hundred years, by being a raving Anglophile. Every three years she travels to England for several weeks. She was there for the coronation of Queen Elizabeth. Her house is filled with photographs. Madge on Waterloo Bridge, Madge at the Trooping of the Colors. Madge at the Tower of London, which was good for a few delicious shudders after she saw Olivier in *Richard III* at the Old Vic. Those poor little princes . . .

Madge closes their bedroom door behind her and walks down the shadowy hall to the living room where the rows of photos, three walls filled with them, are lightly gilded by the rising sun. In the kitchen she uncovers the parakeet cages and sets them all to chirping with little kisses and coos. She runs water into the kettle for tea, turns up the gas, opens a tin of imported shortbreads, settles herself at the table in the breakfast nook where, the night before, she laid out her pens and linen stationery on the writing board. Thoughtfully nibbling on a biscuit, Madge looks out the bow window and sees Shannon Hill, who is trudging across her, Madge's, backyard in pajamas, carrying a large stuffed animal and a flowered pillowcase in her two hands. A real job of work for Shannon, judging from the awkward way that she—and her face all fiery red from exertion. Except for the large gray strip of tape that appears to cover—

Madge is up so quickly the opened bottle of India ink goes teetering around the table, but it doesn't spill. The next thing she knows she has banged open the screen door and is getting a really good look at Shannon. And the smell of blood fouls the still morning air.

Blood on her pajamas, the pillowcase. Her hands, feet, *hair*. So bedraggled and gamey she is like a shot rabbit. What's that dangling from her neck? A piece of clothesline? More clothesline binds Shannon's blood-caked hands together. There is a look of dreadful numbed earnestness in her eyes. Clutching the tubby blue stuffed animal with the floppy ears and long trunk—Madge recognizes Elefunk, which Shannon has had since she was four years old. Madge has seen the child oh so many times, sitting in the old squeaky glider beneath their persimmon tree, rocking the glooms and meanies away with her dear Elefunk.

"Shannon! Oh God! Oh bless you sweetheart! What have you—"

Her eyes go to the silent, familiar house Shannon has left in haste, and back to the soaked, lumpy pillowcase. Shannon keeps coming, determinedly, but with a stumbling, palsied gait, and Madge, quaking head to toe, reaches out. Screaming now. Just ripping up and down the neighborhood like a keening buzz saw, leaving not a soul in his bed. Only Shannon fails to respond. She collapses in a soft heap by the back steps and lies there wrenched by tremblings. Clutching her pillowcase, and Elefunk.

(When they pulled the layers of tape off they found she had bitten her tongue with sharp canines, puncturing it sixteen times.

(By the time they coaxed the pillowcase away from Shannon they'd already been inside and had a good idea of what she'd gathered up, brought with her from the house.

(She gave up her brother Chapman's head and right arm—severed just above the elbow—but she wouldn't let go of Elefunk. Shannon would have killed anyone who tried to separate her from Elefunk, or died in the attempt.)

Flaps retracted, gear up. The Piper Aztec takes off from the Emerson airport in a pink-and-azure dawn, heading west. At the controls, Robert McLaren, slowly bleeding to death internally from a rip in his liver. It can take as long as four hours before, body cold, brain an inert gray lump, fully depatterned, he ceases to function altogether. He has an inkling of this. So little time left, no one to care, he has failed in an act of courage and daring and must now improvise with what remains of his mental vigor. Meanwhile blood rises slowly in his throat like sap in a tree and he continues to sponge it from his tongue and lips. Already accustomed to the heat, the slickness, the harsh carbolic taste of it. The unexpected thirst it causes. Unaccustomed to the frustration of work not completed. Shannon lives. The powerful symphonic poem he was in the act of composing, the great work that could unite him with his mother at an intersection of space and time mathematically implicit in the music, revealed *only* by the music, may be irretrievable.

He coughs. Can't help himself. Blood sprays the instrument panel in front of him.

Perry.

Who was he? Nothing but a "dirty trick" they'd played on him. His father's and his grandfather's idea. Like the time they came to him, all smiles, and coaxed him out of his room and drove him to the place where they did the shock-thing. Oh, again and again until the music was gone, it took him years to figure out a way to get it back, bloodletting enjoyable of itself but not the essential thing. What was the use of lamenting? Forget treacherous people and "dirty tricks." The music hovering in the air above Shannon's head, swoop down, gather it in, set a course for zero-starlight, mother-home.

Looking down, Rob tries to decide where he is. Photographic memory, instant recognition of terrain, landmarks. He's too far west already, the city behind him, wishbone intersection of silver railroad tracks enclosing a towering white grain elevator. Rob banks left.

There's the interstate, coming to an abrupt end at a vast plowed field. Road graders, ready-mix trucks, gangs of men at work on an unpaved mile. He is flying at a thousand feet. Remembering the house at 298 West Homestead. The thick stands of trees all around. Tricky. He will have to dive almost straight down toward the front of the house to hit the bedroom in which he left her. Explode into it at better than one-hundred-fifty miles an hour, obliterating them both. It's a tremendous idea. He's overwhelmed by the gutsiness.

the cavalier brilliance of his plan. He can see Dabney Hill smiling at him (a lot of gum exposed where he removed his bridge before retiring) high up on the bedpost. *Kamikaze. Those were the Nip suicide pilots. They'd load up with munitions and dive straight for your ship.* In a microsecond he will have the music back, complete in all its shadings, crescendoes, significance. He will have pleased God with an act of supreme courage, and God will give him back his mother.

Circling, the sun coming into his eyes like a slowly flooding, golden river, Rob reaches for aviator's sunglasses and puts them on. The nose of the Piper Aztec is a little too far down into the sun; must pull up. There. Eastbound, back to town. He follows the highway toward the spire of the First Presbyterian Church, Shannon's neighborhood. A few cars and trucks in transit below. Banking right; the cockpit is filled with blazing, celestial light. He is cold, and quivers from time to time, little tremors of mortality. *How much time?* But already he sees the Hill house as his plane continues around to the right over West Homestead. Just two blocks away; but what's that?

Pulsating red lights, for one thing, mounted atop police cars racing, one behind the other, from the center of town toward

West Homestead. And people—on their lawns, in front of and behind the Hill house. Pajamas, robes, just out of their beds. They've found out. *Perry*. Chopped him smartly how many times, in the back, across the arm, across the stomach? The left arm just there by ribbons, a bit of sinew, *how could he have survived*? An alarm goes off in the cockpit: stalling speed. Robert grabs some sky, sobbing in his frustration. *If they've been inside the house, they've got her out*. But he must be sure, and circles again. A few people looking up at the airplane above their heads. Necklace of little faces minted in mild sunlight. He reaches for binoculars, circling around by the church one more time. Focuses on the backyards, and, from a blur of green and shadow, Shannon becomes visible. She is surrounded, protected. Rob has a few moments to make up his mind. Other faces turning up, they are looking his way. He senses a radiant anger that makes him timid. If he attempts to crash-land on top of Shannon now, they'll all have enough warning; and besides, the trees are a formidible barrier, the angle is all wrong.

Another moment. Now he sees her, she is looking too. A trembling in the air, her face blanks out. Hopeless. There will be no music this morning. Leaving Shannon to her destiny, he applies more power, gains altitude. Flies west, whining impotently, to the snow cliffs of the Rockies, motherland.

(And then she would take off her lacy, crisp white white bra, all chubby rosiness beneath, beguiling. Liking him to look at her. Doesn't know how he's supposed to feel. Like a thief. Steal glimpses, later touches. Steal what is precious from the father, the crime will be known. The father will kill him.)

At fourteen thousand feet, circling, half-frozen in the thin blue air, he asks, *Will this do?*

The vast, basking body of the mountains; the dark and terrifying thicket. Surely she will not let the father kill him.

Unbuckles and unlocks the door, but it is held fast by the pressure of the wind. He puts the plane into a yaw against the wind and is able to force the door open. Holding on to the seat, he sets one foot outside on the wing, and the other, surrenders to the slipstream.

Impact with the tail assembly breaks nearly all of the bones in his lower body. He doesn't lose consciousness, and, at last in free-fall, Robert McLaren has his answer.

It won't do.

Face-up in the sun, a trembling in the air; exposed within clouds, she is smiling at him as if at a secret jest.

There's no God, Robbie. There's just us.

And still he hears nothing. Not even his own screams.

What scares you?

(Dark where she is. But she understands that it's almost time to get up. She's had enough of being a slug-a-bed. And quite enough, thank you, of this place, although it cannot be said they have treated her unkindly here. In a way she will be sad to leave.)

What scares you?

(That question again. She has to smile. She has never felt so good. There is no fear.)

"I'm not afraid of anything, Dr. McLarty."

Good girl. Then there's no reason for you not to open your eyes.

"Well—"

Something's still bothering you.

(Still smiling, but her breath is caught, she can't squeeze air past her throat.)

Take your time, Suzy.

No. I'm Shannon. Suzy's getting married today, remember? And then she's going away and we probably won't see her or hear from her again.

Oh, yes, I did forget. Well, it's going to be a very important day, isn't it? But before you

get up, and have your shower and some breakfast, would you like to tell me what's on your
mind?

"I—I need to know for sure."

That's understandable. You need to
know who it was. You're not afraid of him any
more—

"Huh-uh."

But you want to know, so you'll never
have to think about it again.

"As long as I live."

As long as you live. Well, Shannon. All
you have to do is ask me. You know I've never
lied to you.

"You've never lied to me. Dr. McLarty—
it was—Perry. Wasn't it?"

Of course. Perry did it. Now you can put the tragedy out of your mind forever, Shannon.

Forever.

Time to rise and shine. Open your eyes, my dear. There's so much to do before you're ready to leave.

(Still dark. But some distance from her there is a shaft of light like morning sunshine that hurts, just a little, causing tears. Someone is there, standing just outside the scintillating white light: the familiar, rumpled, potbellied figure of Dr. McLarty. It has been a long time since she wanted or needed the gift of sight, but this vision is totally reassuring. To be free of fear, now and forever—she trembles, ecstatic.)

Remember, Shannon. Things to do.

"Oh—sure."

It's important to finish the strip. Can't just leave Suzy dangling. We want to get her married off, good and proper. By the way, who's the lucky guy?

"You know, her boyfriend. Robbie."

That's right. We've heard all about him, but we haven't actually seen Robbie yet. So he's going to be in the strip today?

"Well, he has to be. They're getting *married*."

Shannon, I can hardly wait. Oh, there's one thing—call it a favor to me.

"Sure, Dr. McLarty."

There's someone I'd like for you to invite to the wedding. A special friend. You don't mind?

"No. What's his name?"

Donald Carnes.

"If you describe him to me, I can draw him."

I know you can, Shannon. You're so wonderfully talented.

They are trekking now through the cold darkness of the former Woodrow & Lavont department store, on the trail of the elephant that can be heard, from time to time, trumpeting hugely and with a certain note of sorrow; but its whereabouts are still a mystery. There seems to be no end to the floorspace, it expands with their explorations as the savannah of the Masai expanded to the keen senses of the hunter-tracker.

"*Resase modja*, the Somali gunbearers called me. This is an honor not easily won in Africa."

"What does it mean?" Don asks stuffily, raising his handkerchief to his nose to suppress a sneeze.

"'One bullet.' All I ever needed for a kill."

"I don't remember reading that in *Green Hills of Africa*."

"At the time, I was too modest to mention it."

"Not that it may be a very useful skill here. Even if you were carrying a gun, I mean."

"We may wish I had the .450 Express, or even the .303," Papa says, "if we happen to suddenly come across *Bwana temba* in an unsociable mood."

"You mean the elephant? We're not getting any closer. We must be going in circles."

"Don't talk balls. I never lacked for direction."

Papa stops abruptly, thrusting out the torch to lengthen the limits of his vision.

They both hear it: a chilly slithering in the air. Liquid. Lubricious. But nothing is visible in the dark beyond the unsteady nimbus of the torch that is slowly eating itself up.

Don's teeth begin to chatter.

"It's a school of them," Papa says. "Directly ahead of us. To hell with it. We'll have to find another way."

"School of *what*?" Don says worriedly; a little more fright, another creaking notch on the rack.

"You'll know when you see one. Over here."

"I'm totally lost! You acted as if you knew where you were going! We've got to find stairs—something—some way to get to—"

"We could use a rummy guide," Papa admits. "But they're making themselves scarce tonight. I wonder—look out, Carnes!"

For a fraction of a second Don sees the thing, torpedo-shaped and a rusty-gray color with stupid frog's eyes and a snout like a long tightly twisted vine, slipping down with a luminous spinning motion out of the dark and aimed at his head. Papa reacts, thrusting the torch in the intruder's path, diverting it as fast as the eye can blink. Going by it makes a kind of silly high-pitched brassy sound, like a musical air horn. Only a few sparks are left in the air above Don's head as Papa drags him away with the other hand. The windy slithering sounds diminish with their retreat.

"My God, that was—"

"*Mais certainement.*"

"But they don't exist!"

"Everything exists, at this time and in this place. Everything that's been in her mind since the massacre. Woodrow and Lavont is teeming again, Carnes, and not just with high-priced budgies in gilded cages. Needle-nosed air sharks. Kittywamps. Forquidders, fetish-foxes and venomous smews."

"*Tuck Tiller's Incredible Best-Ever Surprise Birthday Party. Williwaw Wilkins and the Moonboggle.* Jesus, that one looked like—"

"Wouldn't fit in here, moonboggles are commonly seven-and-a-half stories tall, not counting their topknots. Most of your beauty's creations are harmless, and none of them are good to eat. It's not the children's stories we have to worry about, it's The Strip."

"The Tafts of Roseboro, Kansas?"

"Sure. Typical, well-scrubbed, whole-some, mindless middle-American family meets Beelzebub. Might have a fighting chance, ordinarily, but not if it's on his turf. Hear that?"

"Yes. Drums?"

"Don't think so." They pause, pondering the muffled, measured metallic roar. Then there is a powerful, prolonged, gut-wrenching, nosy-trumpet solo.

"That is one goddamned pissed-off *tembo*," Papa says admiringly.

"What's going on?"

"We will make tracks to find out. Not that way!"

"Why?"

"Venomous smew country. I can smell the buggers."

Another detour, Don waxing impatient and evermore frightened, for Shannon's sake. The torchlight is low and red, barely enough light to cover the two of them. Shufflings, low breathing in the dark. A metallic rattling, as if something is trying to get out of a cage. They are all cave dwellers, aware of, uneasy with one another. Papa pauses to light the second torch. After a few moments of slow-curling flame it flares up. Don sees, off to their left, a startled begrimed face, swaddled, rotund figure. Knit cap, shoulder-length gray hair as blunt and shaggy as an old whisk broom. A woman? She is pushing a shopping cart across the concrete floor, possibly the rattling noise he heard, distorted by the vast emptiness of this place and the state of his nerves. The cart is heaped with bags, papers, cartons. Her

230

earthly possessions. She attempts to with-draw, but the wheels of the cart won't go in reverse, and it's too heavy for her to drag.

Papa holds the torch out, the better for them all to see. She snarls at this intrusion.

"Where are we off to, daughter?" Papa asks calmly.

"I have a right to change my place of residence when I get the fidgets."

"But it's raining out."

"When it's time to go, it's time to go."

The elephant sounds off again; she hunches her shoulders until they hide her ears and looks craftily at Papa.

"You heard that."

"I believe I did. Where is he?"

"She. That is to say, whatever it is, it's got no balls. Not like them that I seen at the zoo, when I lived fancier uptown."

"She. The female of the species. But do you know where—"

"Upstairs. Where there's all sorts of goings-on."

"For instance?"

"Would you have a dollar on you, mis-ter?"

"No."

Her mouth turns down vehemently. She rattles her shopping cart at them.

"You're blocking traffic."

"I have," Don says. "maybe two dollars."
He's looking, by the flickering light, at something that moves in one of the bags in the shopping cart. A nudge here, a nudge there, trying to make room for itself. His skin crawls.

"We could use a guide, daughter," Papa says. "We need to get to the goings-on. Without delay."

"Don't look at me. It's not worth *my* life." She stares suddenly at the black garbage bag wiggling on top of her pile in the cart, then leans over, protectively placing both arms on it. They hear a muted howl. Don's skin crawls faster over his store of ice-cold blood.

"What's that you've got in the bag, daughter?"

"Don't 'daughter' me, Mr. Whiskers! To the best of my knowledge I was never conceived of your loins. If you knew who I was, you'd have some respect. I lived thirty years in a triplex at 600 Park Avenue. My husband was Mr. Hamilton. If you haven't heard of him, too bad for you. Oww!"

She jumps back suddenly as something like a head pops up from the shiny plastic bag. Dark, rugged head, snappy bright eyes. Almost like a hyena pup but the wrong color: a vivacious, electric green. The woman regroups quickly, wrestles it back down into

232

the bag and holds the bag tight, like the valve of a balloon, in one fist. She sneaks a look at them.

"You didn't see that."

"More goings-on?" Papa inquires politely.

Don draws a heavy breath. "I think," he says, "it was a gadzook."

"Sure it was a gadzook."

The woman laughs derisively. "I've had my fill of you two crazy bums," she declares. "Out of my way, I'm going to the zoo! It's finders-keepers in this world. I found it. And they'll pay me for it. Enough to bargain for my late husband's remains. They've got him in the greenhouse, until the railroad bonds mature. Orchids growing on his grave. There are some that will say it's a nice touch. I'm not fooled. I never held Mr. Hamilton's siblings in high regard, that's for sure. If you live long enough, all of your suspicions about human nature are bound to be confirmed. But will the *Times* print my letters? What's your hunch?"

"Daughter, I think I am becoming very fond of you."

She wipes a hand across her nose. "That 'daughter' stuff," she simpers, and shrugs. "Elevator's no good to you. It's not running. You might not want to be on it if it was."

"There are elevators, and there are elevators."

"I get your meaning."

"We have to be on the right one, and in damned short order."

"Then your best bet's the stairs. All the way to the sixth floor. It's probably left already, though. The doors are closed. No more room."

"How many in the wedding party?"

"The *what?*" Don says.

"Everybody I know, from the first floor on up. Pup and Smokie Joe and Vashti and The Hook. None of those noddies in the shooting gallery, who can't stand on their own two feet. Speaking of undesirables. Let them come out of it for a couple minutes, they will cut your throat if they think you have a buck in your shoe."

"What wedding?" Don says.

"Expect there'll be room for two more," Papa says thoughtfully. "Don? Pony up two dollars."

The woman ties a knot in the garbage bag and rummages deeper among her possessions.

"Pony up three, you get this."

She holds out a child's plastic play-sword—gilt cutlass handle, curved blade—that looks as if the child had teethed on it.

Don, wallet in hand, hesitates. Papa gives him a sharp look. The woman is miffed. She swishes the flexible sword through the air.

"I wouldn't go where you're going without it," she says ominously.

"Why?"

"It's the sword of Damocles. Your ignorance is no reflection on me."

For a couple of moments Don thinks he is going to start screaming. Then he tears most of the cash from his wallet and thrusts it at the woman. Her muddled but oddly cherubic face lights up; she hands over the sword and turns her back on them, finding a safe place for the fistful of dollars beneath her shabby outer garments.

"Now take us to Shannon!" Don demands of her.

"Hold on, hold on," she mumbles, but at last is satisfied with the disposition of her loot. The gadzook is carrying on inside the garbage bag, threatening to topple it from the cart. She swats the bag with an open hand. "Settle down!" To Papa she says, "Follow me," then glances hard at Don, as if disapproving of the way he is holding the sword, by the raggedly chewed blade instead of the handle.

"I could give you a hand with the cart, daughter."

"No help needed, Mr. Whiskers."

As they trudge along she murmurs and chuckles to herself. In addition to other sounds of the dark—rhythmic swamp-grunts, catcalls, peckings and noodlings—they hear a high, sustained scream. It has power, momentum, but no emotion. Fear, pain, ecstasy, the scream is about none of these basic things. Yet it goes on and on, until Don is grinding the enamel off his back teeth.

"La-la-la-la," the woman sings breathily. "The noddies are restless tonight. I'm betting you don't make it through noddie country."

"What's she talking about?" Don says hoarsely to Papa, who, one hand in a side slit of his sou'wester, the other holding the torch to light the way, is into his own steady trudge and unshared thoughts. He shakes off the question somewhat irritably. Don stumbles on the uneven floor and thereafter concentrates on his footing. He has a raging headache. He is half sick from despair. But in a way he's grateful for physical discomfort, otherwise he could not believe his own senses. If there is room for anomalies in mathematics—and anomalies do exist— there is room for them in life. He does not have to rigorously define the world which he is now experiencing, he must only manage to survive it. The scream again. If it is neither a relief nor a necessity to scream, why do it at all? Don squints in misery and holds his tender head.

They have come to a series of plywood partitions and walkway tunnels like those put up by construction people around the city so that pedestrians won't fall into awesome holes in the earth or be lobotomized by dropped rivets. Smoke from the torch hovers nastily under the low roof, choking Don as he brings up the rear. Left turn, right turn, a long straightaway, where will this end? Poor Shannon. At least it is not Shannon whose screams he must bear: The anonymous sound might not even be human. Some kind of machine. A computer programed to scream, as a joke, when it loses at chess.

The squeaky-wheeled grocery cart is on an incline now. They're going down. Torch-light revealing nothing but the narrow plywood tunnel. Someone has spray-painted what look like political slogans in a middle-European language. Why here? Don thinks of men in cloth caps huddled, smoking tobacco harsh enough to kill the tastebuds, plotting firebombings. The woman sings in a wistfully jocular voice, "Ain't misbehavin'." She knows all the words. Tears come to Don's eyes. He brushes them away, still holding that fool sword. Their footsteps sound more and more hollow. The tunnel ends.

A damp place, paint peeling from the walls, more huge bolted-together iron pipes feeding out of it than from the chambers of a heart.

"That way," she says, and Papa walks around her with the torch to better examine a series of rusted iron steps going from platform to platform up into the dark of a shaft through which rain comes down intermittently, revealed in silvery streams.

"Why, daughter?"

"It takes you past noddie country, if you know how to be quick and careful. Otherwise, you're in the thick of them. You'll have a sporting chance, anyhow. Well, I'm on my way! Don't look for me back here any time soon. First it's the zoo, then I plan to be unstinting in my efforts to funeralize the late Mr. Hamilton."

Papa takes off the slouch hat of his sou'wester and grins widely.

"Our thanks to you, daughter."

He lights her way back to the lip of the tunnel. Don is already on the stairs, looking up, quivering, impatient. "Come on!" This time he leads the way, footsteps clanging, as Papa follows with the torch.

"Look out for surprises," the old hunter says, grunting; they both find it a chore going up, straight up, on the treacherous iron stairs. The light is barely adequate. Rain drips on their heads.

They hear screams, squeals, commotion.

"That's—something else, isn't it?" Don says, breathing hard, a stitch in his side.

"Sounds like an ordinary old porker to me. Probably more than one."

"What—next?"

"Third floor. Keep moving."

"I don't know why—haven't kept up at the gym. Lifetime—member. Shouldn't—neglect myself."

Papa is right behind him, the remains of the torch flaking scraps of hot charred paper at Don's neckline.

"Running out of light. Another minute or two. Speed it up, Carnes."

"I'm not quitting. Your old man—in the boat. With his fish. Wouldn't give up—his fish. That's me. I'm not—giving up Shannon."

"Fourth floor!"

"Listen—"

"Don't stop."

"But I heard—I thought I heard—"

"Yes. The elevator. Just the other side of the stairwell. *Go.*"

Fifth floor.

"Papa!"

"I know. I smell it too."

"Fire!"

"It's either a riot, or a feast. Maybe both. A few more steps, Carnes."

"God—I'm going to pass out."

His eyes are fixed on the door at the landing a few steps away. Then he can't see it any more as he stumbles, slowly lifting a cramped leg. Don thinks, melodramatically, that he is losing consciousness. But it is only the torch, sputtering to a finish in Papa's fist. He hears, beyond a thickness of concrete wall, a rusty creaking, as if the elevator is slipping slowly down within its shaft. He drags himself up the remaining steps and falls against the metal door. Papa hauls him to his feet and out of the way.

"Ready?"

"Few seconds—catch my breath." Don seizes the cramped muscle below his knee, kneading it desperately. Papa is breathing hard too. Hell of a climb, truly. But they've done it. Too late, perhaps; the elevator may be getting away from them.

"Inside," Papa urges him.

"No light. What—will we do now?"

"Plenty of light," Papa says, cracking the

door open. He is right. They are assaulted by howlings, a strong gust of heat and smoke.

"It's those fornicating noddies. They've set the whole sixth floor on fire."

Don, hopscotching, unable to put weight on his still-cramped right leg, goes in after Papa. The sixth floor contains the offices of the Knightsbridge Publishing Company, but they are a shambles. Erect shards of glass partitions appear blood-red in the grungy smoke. Fires blaze in half a dozen containers of the sort used by cleanup crews—large metal cannisters on wheels. Sprinklers have come on in one quadrant of the floor. There are animals everywhere, creatures in the clouded air, haphazard in flight or brawling viciously. Common barnyard pigs. Other, fanciful species Don couldn't name even if he'd had the collected works of Shannon Hill with him for reference. The din is amazing. Rap music from a jam box. Musical horns. Alarm bells. Shrieks of terror and laughter. The computerized scream they've been hearing all through the building.

But they no longer hear the furious trumpet of the bright-blue elephant, which is lying massively and motionless on its side twenty feet away in front of the battered, partly open elevator doors.

"Elefunk!" Don says, tearful in the smoke.

"Do you have money?"

Noddies. A dozen of them, men and women, although Don has to look twice to recognize the sex differential. Men with fervid lips and a certain lean beauty, women who need to shave. They are all thin, tattooed, by one sort of needle or another, luminous as polluted fish except for the spokesman, who is Puerto Rican or West Indian or something, almost a head taller than others in his druggy band. Gold in his teeth and earlobes, hair in bronzy ringlets down to his shoulders. He's wearing a silver lamé jacket and toreador pants. They advance slowly out of the smoke. A third of them with the shakes and mumbles. No threat. But the rest, including the spokes-man, are crudely armed, with jagged fluorescent tubes, scissors, the black blade from a paper cutter.

"Pleeeezzze, some moneys? We doan hurt you. Very much."

"We don't have time for this," Papa warns unnecessarily. "Give them money."

Don has his wallet out. There's not much left. Papa takes the cash from him and flings it into the superheated air. The noddies fall all over themselves and the floor, scrambling for wadded bills, as Papa and Don try to edge by them to the elevator.

"Six dollars? Seven? Thass all?" The spokesman rises up, glaring, snatching one of the dollars from the outstretched hand of a female, who whines at him. He knocks her flat with the back of his hand and brandishes his jagged fluorescent tube. "How much smack will that buy? Huh? You looking like a rich mans to me. Give me more, or I will reep your fockeeng heart out."

"I don't have any more. Here. See?" Don shows him his wallet. "Empty."

"You will be empty in the *cabeza*. I am going to eat your fockeeng brains after I have reep out your fockeeng heart."

Having nothing else in his favor, Don responds by lifting the toy sword. Most of them guffaw at this little joke, except for one noddie, on all fours, who bites him in the ankle like a berserk terrier. He has no teeth, but his gums are cast iron. Don shakes him off anxiously and backs away. He and Papa hear, despite the uproar, the sound of the descending elevator.

"Noooo!" Don wails. But the end of the fluorescent tube is inches from his face, slowly forcing him to the wall and away from the elevator doors.

"Papa! God's sake, do something before this maniac—"

Papa frowns, then puts two fingers between his teeth and whistles as loudly as if he's calling home.

One of Elefunk's leafy ears gives a twitch; her trunk moves like a viper in a basket, curling upward into the black smoke. The noddie who has been leaning against Elefunk's flank feels the tremoring in the large body and looks around slowly.

"Salvador—"

"Shut the fock up, man; I got work to do here."

Don dodges a feint toward his face. Papa whistles again. The noddie with the paper-cutter blade makes an ill-advised move from the side. Papa falls into a boxer's stance and begins to weave and bob. Then his right hand flicks out, once, twice, speed and power like the old days when he was heavyweight champ of the literary world; and the noddie goes spinning to the floor with a brightly tomatoed nose.

Don is not so quick. The broken tube in Salvador's hand takes a small bite out of his cheek. Don loses his balance and stumbles against Papa.

"Damn it, Carnes!"

"Sorry."

The noddies are circling now, little pin-pricks of eyes, clothes that were never new. Pressing in. More broken tubes and paper spikes, some with author's letters still attached, are thrust at them; Don covers his head and face with both arms as an ear is savaged.

Behind the noddies Elefunk rises with a certain exhausted majesty, trumpeting like the solo part in a marching hymn. She stands, perhaps, eight feet at the shoulder. Small for an elephant, but not in this place. She is so wonderfully blue she is almost irridescent: like the Gulf Stream, to Papa's artistic eye, on a hot, calm, cloudless afternoon off Bimini. Her head is split above one eye from the battering of the elevator doors that put her down in the first place; blood trickles from the swollen eye. The other eye is so sad you want to cry with her.

"Give it to them, Beauty! We have an elevator to catch!"

The trunk uncurls and seizes a would-be runaway, stopping him in midstride, lifting him straight and true right through a ceiling panel of acoustical tile, leaving him up there in a welter of plumbing and ductwork with only his skinny, writhing legs visible. Another noddie is lashed across the butt and double-somersaults over the floor into the thickest cloud of smoke. Blood rolls down one side of Elefunk's face, tears down the other. Papa cheers, then seizes the distracted Salvador by the lapels of his clinquant jacket and begins bumping him with his burly chest, back and back until the trunk of the elephant comes snaking down over Salvador's shoulder.

"All yours, Beauty."

Salvador is lifted with a shriek and held suspended for a few moments while Elefunk makes a decision about him. Then she plods across the floor to where a cannister is ablaze and drops him butt-first into it. He fits like a cork in a bottle. He screams and screams.

"The fire will die from lack of oxygen," Papa says. "But his balls should be well-roasted by then."

"The elevator, Papa!"

"I know. Elefunk, help us!"

The blue elephant, weeping buckets, returns, her large head rolling unsteadily.

"The doors," Papa says, lifting one floppy ear to speak directly and without interference. Elefunk blinks her good but tearful eye. She has long, curly lashes.

"For Shannon," Don says passionately.

The thick metal clamshell doors, heavily dented by Elefunk's battering, are inches apart. Blackness beyond. Elefunk raises her trunk and inserts it into the opening. She trembles. Then she brings all of her strength to bear on the lower door, forcing it down an inch, another inch.

"Oh, Beauty," Papa says sympathetically, her ear still in his hand. "Thou art Magnificence. Thou art truly the Great One of all *tembu*. I celebrate thy Strength and Spirit. There is no greater Beast. You will do this thing. You are the best of the many brave creatures of the forest and plains. God knew what he was doing when he made you. A little farther, please. He made many with cunning and heart, but only noble *temba* has a soul."

With a shudder and roar the big door slams down.

"Carnes! Hop aboard!"

"Papa, it's not there! The elevator's not—"

"I know that! I hear it moving. It's down there in the shaft, you have to jump!"

"Oh, now, wait a—"

"Jump!"

"I—"

Something smooth and hard like the fleshy nozzle of a fire hose thumps him solidly in the small of the back and Don goes flying out into the gusty cold void of the elevator shaft, somehow not tumbling, just falling feet first for what seems twice the time for a death sentence. In reality only a couple of seconds pass before he lands, hard but on his feet, on the roof of the slowly descending elevator.

"Look out below, Carnes!"

Don scrambles between greasy vibrant cables, looking back and up as Papa jumps and Elefunk trumpets a farewell. Safe for the moment, Don thinks bitterly of himself, *Didn't have the nerve. As usual. Well, shit. When are you going to get it together?* Because the noddies were nothing but feckless clowns compared to what he must soon face: the Axman himself. And how long can he count on Papa's courage and resourcefulness to back him up?

Still holding on to that stupid toy sword. Almost like a pacifier. He looks at Papa in the meager light from the sixth floor, now more than twenty feet above their heads.

"What—what do we do now?" Hates himself for having to ask. *Use your canoodle, Carnes.* He has an inspiration before the winded Papa can reply.

"There must be a hatch cover; some sort of emergency exit from the—"

The elevator is moving perceptibly faster.

"Found it!"

The hatch is about three feet square. But he can't locate a handle, and around the edges there is grease and grime, the accumulation of decades, hard as old caulking. He would need a pry bar to get the cover off. He looks up in frustration and fear, a trickle of blood on one cheek.

"Papa, I—"

Papa's eyes look yellow in the dark shaft. He stares unwinkingly at Don.

"Use the sword."

"It's a toy!"

The elevator is gathering speed; Don has to swallow his heart, rude knocking thing, and swallow it again like a wet apple from a tub. He looks down, then jabs sharply with what is left of the point of the plaything sword to demonstrate his feelings of futilty. And somehow he finds a soft spot, the blade slips in between the hatch cover and the elevator roof. He bears down reflexively on the handle of the sword and feels the hatch move up.

Papa reaches over with both hands and hurls the cumbersome hatch cover away.

"Go!"

Don thinks, *Axman*. It's enough to fry the roots of his hair. And he thinks, *Shannon*. So this it. His moment of truth. He can feel Papa's breath on him, as steamy and intimidating as a bull's breath. He looks down into the elevator for a long moment, but he can't see anything. He swings his feet into the hole, takes a deep breath, lets it out in a full-throated shriek of bravado as he drops.

The elevator, when Don hits the floor below, seems to go into free fall. Don rolls over twice, holding the toy sword, until he comes up against a wall. He is still screaming like an unblooded soldier thrust into battle, adrenaline a bombshell in the brain, a fiery tonic for the survival instinct. He expects the worst—an ax blade flashing swiftly out of the dark, beheading stroke—but is not paralyzed by his expectations. He thrashes everywhere around him with the silly toy in his hand (yet there is weight and a graceful balance to it he has not been aware of before), until Papa comes thumping down in oilskins to join him.

"Watch it, Carnes! You almost took my arm off."

"With this?" Don says incredulously. He lowers the sword, breathing deeply, eyes big as doorknobs as he strains to see. The elevator, picking up more speed, is rumbling hellbent in the shaft, and that's not the worst thing Don is aware of in these moments of developing calamity.

"Shan! **Shannon**! Oh God! Papa—she isn't here!"

"I know that."

"We're going to crash!"

"That also is a matter that has not escaped my attention," Papa says, picking himself up off the floor and dusting his knees.

"You don't have to worry! You can go back to wherever the hell it is you came from! But what's going to happen to *me*?"

"You've handled yourself pretty well up to now. You'll be able to handle that too."

The elevator is buffeted as it falls, there is a high keening sound and some metallic snappings and poppings as if tough cable is parting. A wild, nasty screech of metal wheels on rails. Don senses demolition, jagged edges of shattered floor thrust smoking through all the vital organs of his body; he cups one hand over his testicles, forlornly, and closes his eyes.

As if from a sudden change of direction, an almost right-angle turn at an unbelievable speed, he is lifted from his feet and thrown weightlessly but violently from one side of the elevator to the other. His forehead smacks the wall, and as he rebounds with a hard grunt of pain all motion ceases except for a gentle rocking that nevertheless upsets his equilibrium and makes him nauseous.

"Papa," he mutters thickly, "what happened?" His feet cross and he falls.

Lying there face-up and gagging a little on the bitterness in his throat, he feels the elevator picking up speed again, and he is almost dead certain they are now going sideways. He is also too weak and shocked to lift a finger. He has broken out in a cold sweat. Their speed is tremendous, but Don hears few sounds: the light creakings of the floor beneath him and, more distantly, far beyond the elevator walls, a surging wind or, perhaps, surf toiling endlessly on a beach. Pleasant. He feels no fear. He cannot remember what fear is like. Is death so uncomplicated? Some warmth creeps up from his feet as if he is a saint at a stake. He closes his eyes. He is not aware of the moment when the elevator comes to a full stop.

But the opening of the doors jolts him; he sits upright in a flood of daylight.

"My God! Where—?"

Someone crosses between him and the light. That familiar burly figure, the turtleneck sweater and white beard shapely as a petrel's breast.

"It ain't Grover's Corners."

"Papa!"

The elevator shudders delicately, like a great box kite.

"Better get out of here. We're running late. Probably missed the wedding."

Don rises slowly. Momentary dizziness. The wedding again? Something heavy in his right hand. He looks at it in the welcome flood of light. It's only the toy sword with the chewed blade. But different, somehow. Certainly a lot heavier. He feels good, holding it. Capable and almost confident.

"Where's Shannon?"

"Suppose we find that out."

Shielding his sensitive eyes with the other hand, Don walks out of the elevator onto solid ground. He assumes. He can't see all the way to his feet. There's a wind blowing, hard; he is buffeted. The air around him seems made up equally of light and fog. Zero visibility. And the barometer must be low, wherever this is: he can feel storm pressure on his skin.

"What—uh, which way—?" Papa, a few feet from him, has already lost dimension, is dissolving. This is hard on Don's new-found confidence.

"Just keep up."

The wind soughs in Don's ears; but if there's such a strong wind, how can there be fog? He pauses, bends down, touches—hmm, clipped grass. That's reassuring. He plucks a piece and tastes it. Juicy greenness. Papa is a shadow ahead of him. Don hurries.

Now there is a shape that he can recognize in the paleness: the trunk of a tree. Papa pauses beside it. The fog is thinning. The wind's velocity lessens. They can see more trees, shrubs, a fence, a garden plot enclosed by chickenwire. Gopher traps outside the chickenwire.

Gopher traps?

"Papa, this is—"

"Kansas, bub."

He sees the house. He has been here before, on a melancholy quest.

"Shannon's house!"

"This is where it all happened."

"I know! My God. What time is it? *When* is it?"

"You can't expect me to know everything," Papa grumbles. "Maybe it's just the right time. The wedding's over, but the guests are still here . . ."

"What are you talking about? There's nobody—" Don finds he must shout. There's less fog but the wind is roaring, leaves are flying through the air against a sky green as pond scum. Air pressure hurts his eardrums. He sees a light in the house, moving like a will o' the wisp. Brighter than starshine, fainter than the sun. The clotheslines are hung with flapping sheets.

"That includes the guest of honor! At the groom's request!"

"Axman!"

Papa nods. "He's inside!" They are both

shouting now. The sheets on the line crack like pistol shots.

"Let's go!"

"I'll never make it! Up to you to save your Beauty, Carnes!"

"You've got to come with me!"

"I'm with you! For now! But the cyclone's coming! Get in the house!"

"Can't hear you!"

Papa pushes him, hard. Don stumbles into the midst of the billowing sheets. They look as if they haven't been washed. Then he sees that each one contains a charcoal drawing. Portraits. Friends, neighbors, of the Hills of Emerson, Kansas. Shannon's work. Men wearing their Sunday coats and ties, women in spring finery. And a few who look as if they dwell in niches of the New York subways, bundled up like Eskimos in an arctic night. Bizarre guests at a postnuptial lawn party. They press in on him, one thick smothering layer after another. There is a babble in his head, small talk, mildly off-color jokes suitable for Rotarian lunches and occasions such as this. He can't breathe, he's perspiring heavily. Then he realizes it isn't perspiration. Some of the sheets are wet. Wet with sopped-up blood from unimaginable butchering-beds.

Horrified, he fights his way clear of the

embracing sheets; sticky and smeared with blood like a warrior on his last legs, he steadies himself in the fierce wind. Looking back, he gestures with the sword in his hand for Papa, who doesn't move. Old Hummingbuffer's grinning, but stressfully, something seems to be wrong. Suddenly he begins to shrink in a peculiar, sideways, crumpled manner, as if he is no more than a drawing himself, on a piece of paper someone has decided to dispose of.

The last thing Don sees is the crinkled ball of that indomitable head, the lasting grin; then, all but weightless, Papa goes skimming off in the high wind until he is no more than a spot, a steadily dwindling black hole in the freakish, ominous sky.

If it could happen to Papa, then—

The light he has seen, flashing here, flashing there in the forbidding house, is steadier now; Don feels it focused on him, throwing his shadow four ways at once against the flapping, wailing, ghostlike sheets on the backyard lines. His breath is trying to escape his lungs like a panicky little bird. He feels mercilessly scrutinized, mocked by a devil. There is a lightness to his bones, no familiarity of flesh within his clothes. The wind is sucking him right out of his shoes. Like Papa, he begins to crease and fold, trivially to crumble.

He holds up the sword—or, perhaps, the sword holds his hand up, Don isn't sure—which repeats the light like a metallic mirror until the light withdraws inside the dark, tight house. Don no longer feeling flimsy as the paperboy, and once again secure in his shoes. Holding out the sword also shuts down the wind between him and the house, where the dark turns to a red as mournful as dawn in hell and then to dark again; and a face appears in one window, like a ghost in iodine. The face of a rival, an enemy. He can't make it out very well. But he's not afraid of what he sees. With the lull in the wind he enjoys a calm space around his heart. Shannon, after all, is his through investiture, the giving and receiving of love. The Axman, *malhechor*, claims solely by terror. The little toy sword he disdained is vibrating like a tuning fork from a secret vigor, energy pouring off it and causing the tip of his nose to tingle. "Made in Taiwan" is stamped on the blade, which is still some kind of inexpensive vinyl and wouldn't cut through a stick of butter. He knows this. He has no wind and can't fight, never did learn how. Logically, he has no chance. He knows this too. But he could not be crumpled, blown away like Papa, the tiniest of bangs in the universe. According to up-to-date insights provided by computer mathematics, much of the universe cannot be accounted for. It is simply missing. Toy swords made in Taiwan do not stop the wind. This is bad mathematics. Obviously the Taiwanese knew something when they made this particular sword, something they have not let on to the world at large. Just as obvious, it has served him as an entry to one of those islands of the missing universe, like a complicated musical code or the pattern of blood vessels in an eye. Don chuckles. He is calm. The windows of the house, the doors, are opening. He hears stentorian music. Martial, Wagnerian, but nothing he is familiar with. His heart starts up from a swoon like a prodded steer. *Let's go*, he says to himself.

He is walking up to the back porch. Behind him the cyclone rages, shedding light in artillery bursts. It is Emerson, Kansas, and it is not.

In Shannon's house they are all dead, or else they never were.

He goes from room to room looking for corpses, finding nothing but neatly made beds and hand-embroidered for-show pillows. Home-sweet-homilies. Invocations.

There is nothing to see in the bride's bedroom but her white shoes, and red teardrops on each shoe.

"Shannon?"

The music plays like someone's rage.

"Shannon, answer me!"

The toy sword is sulking in his hand.

Down dusty back steps to the kitchen, where no one has made coffee in ages, and the roast on the silver plate on the table is too old and dry for mice to eat.

The house shakes as if from a bomb. It trembles in sorrow.

More steps, down.

Petals on the steps from the bride's bouquet: forget-me-nots.

Her small footprints luminous as snail tracks.

"Shannon, I love you."

For lack of anything else to say.

She's there in the cellar.

Barefoot, a little careworn, but alive.

He is there too, debonair in cutaway and silk cravat, leaning on the cheated ax as if waiting for an audience.

The music is as powerful, as stifling as the depths of a river.

Shannon is seated on the edge of a large and curving petit-point chair, precariously, as might be imagined, in a wedding gown full as a flowering tree. Her arms are extended to the low curved back of a similar chair, her head forward like a swan's and resting on her arms, baring all of her lovely neck. She doesn't look, to Don, to be a day over sixteen.

The love inside him is a great blundering thing, like an ape on a chain.

Axman is as youthful as Don imagined him to be, although there were never any clues: fresh, highly colored by the infection of homicide.

In his free hand he has another of Shannon's drawings of Don, which he holds cannily propped against his breast like a door-to-door salesman. Getcher *Time*!

Donald B-for-Burnside Carnes, Man of the Year.

A tingling in Don's right arm, as if he has plugged the toy sword into a wall socket.

"It won't work," Don tells him, the flare-up of bravado like a torch in the cellar dimness. "Also, frankly I think your music stinks. It's not original. You never had any talent and you never will."

Axman begins slowly to crumble the page, enjoying his mastery. Don feels a contraction of gut and muscle but doesn't flinch and the sensation ebbs. The Taiwanese sword is twitchy, like a cat at a mousehole.

Shannon slowly lifts her head in hazy wonder.

Axman tosses the half-wadded drawing to the floor and takes a step back, raising in a smooth effortless lethal motion the prodigious ax. It has never failed him. Glowering half-moons that throw off death like radium. Shannon trembles in her wilting wedding gown. The house above their heads cracks like a brittle walnut shell. The wind flies in, filled with dust from an opened grave. Her face is parched by the draught, her rouged lips look stark as graffiti on a church wall. Don stands firm as the Axman cometh, blades windmilling fancily to trim his flesh and dress him down to his humble bones.

The Axman gloating over his catch.

"Finished! Finished! Finished!"

"Damn right," says Don, and the little sword flies up, marvellous in its dance, in the precision of its mathematics—flies against the trajectories of the ax and bewilders them, undoes the equations of butchery by splitting the ax through the handle and to the wrist, leaving fingers here and fingers there on the floor and a gout of blood on Axman's frilly wedding shirt. Don's sword leads him adeptly by the arm, pointedly taking inventory of vital spots, support columns and various low joints while Axman writhes and screams in obligatory partnership, until there are only stumps of him left to do the dance, his eyes are blind as belly buttons, his hair a hive of hardened grave dust.

And at last they rest, while the gathering of Axman by the stellar wind goes on, his pieces distributed according to laws of celestial mechanics Don is too bushed to ponder. Nor can he reckon yet with his own situation.

He's in Kansas. There's a Kansas-size wind blowing, the stuff of tall tales. And Shannon lies on the floor pale as a twisted soda straw, naked as January.

He crawls to her, grateful for even that much locomotion. Gathers her in his arms. Kisses her shriveled lips back to a sweet redness. Her young breasts bloom beneath his hand. At last her eyes open.

"Oh, Shannon. Let's just get out of here. But which way?"

Puzzled, she studies his face as if it is a road map in Cyrillic.

"Thank you. I don't think I need any more help. I can make it the rest of the way."

"Shannon—it's Don. Wake up!"

"I am awake. Well, sort of." She smiles. Her eyes seeing past him, as if trying to focus on the shimmering edge of a faded, rainy dream, an ice palace in a desert. "But I want to go back to sleep. There's plenty of time. It's Saturday, isn't it? I don't have to get up so early on Saturday."

"Shannon. What's going on? You don't know what I—what we've been through!"

"I don't even know who you are," she says, and yawns contentedly. "But that's okay. I know you won't be here when I wake up again."

"Stop it! Listen to me! He's gone for good now! You're rid of him, Shannon. You never have to think about him again. So there's no reason why we can't be happy—"

Her eyes have closed.

"I'm very happy," she murmurs, begging off. And then, not looking at him, she puts her lips to his cheek.

"'Bye."

"No—no, you can't! Shan, I love you! We're going to be together now! We have to be, that's what this was all about! I saved you from the Axman. Wake up, please, come back! It's me, *Donald*! You've got to *wake up*, beauty!"

The wind is loud and strong. But Shannon lies unruffled in his arms, fair of skin in the strong cocoon of Time, glistening newly like lightning in a bottle. She will smile forever, but no longer for him.

Tears in his eyes. He is lost and knows it. Lost in goddamn Kansas, with nowhere to go, and all the magic he might have expected as his due is worthless, inert, as flat as week-old beer.

The least he can do is put her back in her own bed. He weeps at the thought.

His tears falling on her face as he carries her lightly up the cellar stairs. The toy sword thrust into his belt. But he can't swagger, there is no freebooter in him, only an ice cave, a lonely heart like a pebble covered with snow.

Her room, and he receives a shock. It is pretty much as he imagined it would be, from crime-scene photographs he once looked at. Another shock: there is a body lying curled in pajamas on the floor, wrapped in a chenille spread pulled from her bed. He steels himself, expecting horrors, more blood. But the boy is unharmed. He snores gently, with a slight rasp.

Don lays Shannon on her bed. He dresses her in clean pajamas and smoothes the rumpled hair with her own brush, but he knows nothing will wake her as long as he is there. Should he stay until he is blind from cataracts and deaf to his own heartbeat, she will sleep and have no thoughts of him. They will all sleep.

When he pulls the sheet up to her

breasts Elefunk tumbles out of the folds, one white felt teardrop dangling from a doleful, thickly lashed eye. He puts Elefunk in the crook of Shannon's arm and thinks he sees the slightest change in her expression, a deepening of contentment as she slumbers on.

Chap stops snoring but doesn't wake up when Don lifts him into the bed beside his sister.

As he turns to leave the room his gaze lingers on a framed photograph on her vanity. A good-looking, dark-haired boy in a football jersey. Not just another jock, perhaps. There is a sensitivity about the eyes Don finds appealing. He has inscribed the photograph *To Shannon: the best and the most at Emerson High* and finished with a quotation: *This hour I tell things in confidence/I might not tell everybody/but I will tell you.*

He can't leave the house without checking all the bedrooms. Just to be sure.

So it's Dab and Ernestine first, in rudimentary nightclothes, finishing this night together as they have finished the nine thousand–nights that came before, not decorating their bedposts like horrendous Toby mugs.

Allen Ray breathes peacefully but not through his throat, where the only mark is insignificant, from his own razor.

Now Don has overstayed; he is walking around and around in a museum where he knows all the exhibits by heart.

He no longer hears the wind. Perhaps it is too close to dawn. The house has settled on its old foundation, nails and mortar snug, the refrigerator humming its familiar buzzy song.

He leaves by the backdoor, and it is like passing through an airlock.

Japanese lanterns like multiple suns dangle from the trees in the backyard.

There are no houses beyond the back fence. The neighborhood ends abruptly there, in empty sky and prairie, gold on this windless morning. It is Kansas, or it is not. But there is no other way to go. He does not trouble to look behind him.

He has walked a mile when things begin to look both different and familiar. The chrome yellow of wheatlands is giving way to green thickets, orchard bush. He sees thorn trees in yellow flower. He crosses a clear stream. On the bank the red mud and reeds are heavily trampled. Animal dung covered with camel flies steams in the cool air, not unpleasantly. That, and the tang of game, excites his nostrils, his sporting blood.

Don rubs a hand across his lower jaw. Growth of whiskers there. Almost a beard. Another few days. Then he will shape it. He always knew he had a good face for a beard, but of course they had rules back there, in the actuarial department of New York Life.

His stride lengthens. He's not surprised to find that he's wearing crepe-soled walking shoes suitable for the bush. Also high socks and shorts and a short-sleeved safari jacket from those perennial expedition outfitters Abercrombie & Fitch. He's unarmed, except for his small toy sword, which no man dares make fun of. He has knocked a few men down for daring. The sword will always go with him. It will never be far from his hand at night. No matter what his women have to say about that.

The sun is higher. From his musette bag he takes a bandana, cocks the brim of his Stetson higher and knots the bandana around his head below the hairline so that perspiration won't mist his glasses. The wind is from the west and in his face, swaying almost noiselessly the tall grasses all around him. The game trail is cut like a shallow winding trench through the grass, but smooth and shining like mudpies patted tirelessly by small hands and left to dry in the sun. This is a good country, not too broken, some tough climbing but nothing that will wear a man down.

Ah. He hears one now. Simba's cough, deep and full of anger. Somewhere over the next shaded ridge. His hands tingle. He is walking quickly but making no sound. Even the vanguard of Somali gunbearers jump when they realize he's joined them, and grin in relief. It is only *Resase modja.*

Papa, crouching, the .256 Mannlicher in his right hand, looks back over his shoulder. So does the white hunter beside him.

Papa says in a low voice, "You made excellent time. Baron Blixen, this splendid-looking bastard is my good friend Donald B-for-Burnside Carnes."

Blixen offers his hand. "I've heard so much about you. Delighted you could join the hunt."

"My pleasure," Don says, and kneels. He thrusts out his left hand, and almost immediately his own weapon is there. He senses the nerves of Abdullah, his gunbearer, knock-kneed in flimsy khaki shorts, and touches the black man reassuringly. Then he opens the breech of the Springfield and is satisfied. Clean as a hound's tooth and loaded with five solids, the 220-grain bullets. Power hitters. But he and Papa will need only one shot apiece. They are the best.

"Cotsies are bloody restless," Papa murmurs. "Also they've winded us."

"When they come," Don says, studying the maned lions that are just barely visible at seventy-five yards in the *donga* grass, "they

268

will try to flank us like the good soldiers and hunters they are."

"I wouldn't care for this situation at all," Blixen says thoughtfully, mopping his brow. "If I were with any but you chaps, what?"

"I am highly complimented," Don says, not breaking his concentration. And then he realizes, with the superb hunter's instinct, that the lions are going to charge. Perfectly synchronized, he and Papa cock their rifles. For a moment their eyes meet. They smile.

The gunbearers, brave in their own right but weaponless, have retreated before the anticipated charge. A shout goes up. The grass undulates as if tornadoes are snaking through it. Don returns his attention to the beast surging within his sights. A large male, four hundred pounds or more, capable of breaking a buffalo's neck with a single paw-swipe. Papa's lion is equally large. Such speed and beauty, Don almost hates to pull the trigger. His pulse is racing. His heart is full. He is where he was always meant to be.

"Now!" he says, and the two guns crack as one; birds fly from the dark branches of the baobab trees. The shouts of warning and fear turn quickly to ringing cheers.

Author's Note

Almost all of Perry Kennold's italicized lovelorn musings are from Walt Whitman's *Leaves of Grass*.

This one is dedicated to the Brothers Grimm.

And, of course, it's also for Papa. Who, one likes to think, would have been amused.